LAURENCE YEP

angelfish

G. P. PUTNAM'S SONS · NEW YORK

G. P. Putnam's Sons, a division of Penguin Putnam Books for Young Readers,
345 Hudson Street, New York, NY 10014.

G. P. Putnam's Sons, Reg. U.S. Pat. & Tm. Off. Published simultaneously in Canada.
Printed in the United States of America.

Designed by Sharon Murray Jacobs. Text set in twelve-point Goudy Oldstyle.

Library of Congress Cataloging-in-Publication Data

Yep, Laurence. Angelfish / Laurence Yep. p. cm. Sequel to: The cook's family.
Summary: Robin, a young ballet dancer who is half Chinese and half white, works in a fish
store for Mr. Tsow, a brusque Chinese who accuses her of being a half person and who harbors
a bitter secret. 1. Chinese Americans—Juvenile fiction. [1. Chinese Americans—Fiction.
2. Ballet—Fiction. 3. Racially mixed people—Fiction. 4. Fishes—Fiction.
5. Grandmothers—Fiction.] I. Title. PZ7.Y44 An 2001 [Fic]—dc21   00-062676

ISBN 0-399-23041-6

1 3 5 7 9 10 8 6 4 2

FIRST IMPRESSION

To Sam Sebesta, who loves musicals,
and to Russ MacMath and his Richmond students

1

Beauty and the Beast

For ten minutes, I was on top of the world.

At the end of ballet practice, Madame announced the roles for the next recital, and I was going to play Beauty.

Madame had decided to do the ballet based on Ravel's *Mother Goose Suite, Ma Mère l'Oye*. The ballet begins with the story of *Sleeping Beauty*. When she falls asleep, she dreams of other stories such as *Tom Thumb* and our *Beauty and the Beast*. At the end, when Prince Charming kisses her, she wakes up in the Fairy's Garden. And everyone dances happily ever after.

As we walked along in our sweats after ballet, my friend Amy congratulated me. "You're perfect."

"I hope I don't fall on my face," I said, trying to be modest. "But you'll be a great Tom Thumb. And Leah will make those fairies behave."

"I'm going to crack the whip in that garden," Leah agreed. "I think we should celebrate."

Thomas wagged a finger at me. "Well, no more fried food for you." Thomas was being Thomas as usual. "It's getting harder and harder to lift you. I'm going to need to pump some iron if I'm going to get you off the stage."

I took that personally. "I weigh just the same as always."

Thomas rubbed the small of his back as if it was sore. "Then your center of gravity must be getting lower. I strained my back trying to pick you up."

Leah came to my defense. "Madame got the casting right when she made you the Beast."

For the school recital, Thomas and I were to be Beauty and the Beast. Though we had danced together before, the routines had been nowhere near as complicated as this one. So the last thing I needed was to lose my confidence.

"Don't tease me anymore, Thomas," I warned.

"Or we'll . . ." Amy launched into a vivid Chinese curse.

Thomas turned to me. "What'd she say?"

My own Chinese wasn't as good as hers, so I only picked up on part of it: something about cutting off his head and throwing it into the gutter, where dogs would do unspeakable things to it.

"I couldn't translate it," I said, "but believe me—you won't like it when we do it to you."

Leah rubbed her hands together. "Ooo, sounds good. I'll sell the tickets, and we'll make big bucks."

"Now, now. Let's make up over ice cream." Thomas clapped a hand to his mouth. "Oops. I forgot. You shouldn't eat desserts."

I'd had one too many cracks from Beast Thomas. "Of course I can eat ice cream," I snapped.

Thomas dropped to his knees and clasped his hands together. "Oh, have mercy. Spare this poor back."

"Shut up," I said. I grabbed the first thing I could, which was the strap of my bag, and I swung it.

Thomas, though, was always teasing someone, so he had gotten good at ducking. He dove low to the sidewalk so my bag whipped over his head. Only I didn't have as good a grip on it as I had thought. To my horror, the bag flew out of my fingers and headed straight toward a big plate-glass window.

"Duck!" I shouted, and I fell over Thomas to protect him.

The next moment I heard dozens of little glass bells ringing. Leah was shouting. And then I felt stuff hitting me. Some of it had the weight of pebbles, but others felt as heavy as fist-sized rocks.

"Robin, Thomas, are you all right?" Amy asked. I heard her shoes making crunching noises.

I was still alive, but there were glistening glass shards scattered all over the pavement.

"You could have been killed," Leah said.

I lifted my head slowly and felt small bits of glass cascading from my head down onto my jacket. "Are you okay?" I asked Thomas.

"I can't breathe. You're squeezing me," Thomas wheezed.

"Oh, sorry." I let go of him. "How are you otherwise?"

Thomas straightened. "Fine—thanks to you. That was the dumbest thing—" He stopped and pointed to my cheek. "You're cut."

"How bad?" I asked, putting a hand to my cheek. I wiped away a single drop of blood.

"It's just a little one, but your jacket's all torn," Leah said, fingering a tear.

A voice roared from inside the store. "Who broke my window?"

I just stood there frozen.

A man limped to the now empty window frame. "Who did it?" he growled. He was old and thin and of about medium height. From his broad, round face, I thought he might be a northern Chinese. In his hand, he gripped my rose-colored bag. "Whose is this?"

"M-mine," I croaked.

He closed his eyes. "I should have known it'd be one of you stupid dancers."

Leah stared at him. "How did you know?"

Opening his eyes, he motioned contemptuously toward the back of my head. "Your hair's done up in a bun."

"I can understand why you're upset, but won't your insurance cover the cost of the window?" Leah asked.

He planted a fist on his hip. "Certainly, but my premiums are going to go up. You have to compensate me for that."

"Sure," I said. Suddenly I remembered my mother's threats last night. "I think."

"What's wrong?" Amy demanded, leaning her head close to mine.

I shifted my feet. "I have to buy a new wok. I burned ours."

"You mean *the* wok?" Amy asked, horrified. "My mother would have disowned me. It took her years to get her wok worked in just right."

"Yours is just as black as ours."

Amy clicked her tongue in exasperation as if she were trying to explain something to a little sister. "The black part has all the flavors from past meals."

Leah leaned her head to the side as she tried to re-member. "Let's see. Last week you ruined your mom's sewing scissors."

Amy wagged an index finger at me. "And the week be-fore that, you accidentally erased her soap opera tape."

I couldn't see why my friends were taking my mom's side. "It's just a lot of little stuff," I grumbled. "I still don't see why she should threaten to ground me for my next mistake."

"On weekends?" Thomas asked. He seemed suddenly worried. I don't know if it was so much about losing me as a partner or as a target for his jokes.

"When I say grounded, I mean grounded," I com-plained. "She made it clear I couldn't even go to ballet school during the grounding."

"You'd have to quit the recital," Amy said in a small voice.

Now that he'd realized I couldn't dance with him, Thomas got scared. "But you can't. I don't want to have to get used to having someone else step on my toes."

"My mom was real mad this morning," I said. "This'll make her go ballistic."

Leah got this sly look that always made me worry. Leaning her head near mine, she said from the corner of her mouth, "Only if she finds out."

It was all so hopeless that I felt like crying. In a few seconds, I'd toppled from the top of the world to the bottom. "I can't just go and ask her for the money without telling her."

Leah looked at the others. "Maybe we could help out."

Amy gripped the strap of her bag and smiled apologetically. "I haven't got any money. But you know you could have it if I did, Robin."

Thomas slapped his pockets. "I only have enough for ice cream."

"And I'm broke, too," Leah confessed, chewing her lip.

The old man butted in. "Well, someone's paying for the window. You're lucky you didn't break a fish tank."

I looked around his store. It was dark with lots of aquariums glowing, like small computer screens on which hundreds of bright darts drifted. The sign outside had said it was the Dragon Palace.

Thomas gave me a nudge. "Can't you ask your grandmother for the money?"

My grandmother would give me the money in a second. But then I remembered. "No good. She's saving to take the bus up to Reno with Ah Wing and her friends."

Ah Wing was my grandmother's boyfriend—though they both strongly denied it and blushed whenever anyone teased them.

Leah turned, her eyes scanning the street while she tried to think of a solution. Suddenly her eyes fastened on something. "What if she works it off?" She pointed at a sign taped to the door.

The sign read: PART-TIME HELP WANTED.

Amy gasped. "You can't take a job with a stranger."

Leah rolled her eyes. She was the most daring of us all. "It's not like we don't know where she'll be."

Amy folded her arms. "Well, Robin can't lie to her mother."

Leah could split hairs like the best lawyer. "It's not lying," she argued. "If her mother asks, 'Did you break any windows today?' of course she'll tell her the truth."

Good old Leah. She'd given me a way out. "Sure, then I'd tell her," I agreed. I just hoped she didn't ask.

Leah turned to the angry man. "So, what do you want?"

He rubbed his chin. "I need someone in the late afternoons five days a week from Monday through Friday. That's so I can run errands, go to the bank, pick up supplies, and so on. I pay only minimum wage."

"No Saturdays?" I asked. Our Saturday rehearsals could go on a long time.

"My nephew comes on the weekends," he said.

"I have ballet class right after school. But then I could spend an hour here. Would that be okay?" I asked hopefully.

We worked out a schedule that I thought I could manage. Between the fish store, school, and ballet, I wasn't going to get much sleep.

"How long do I have to work here?" I asked.

He picked a piece of glass from the frame. "Well, three months would do it."

My heart sank. "Three months."

He threw the glass onto the floor. "Maybe you'd better just go home and have your parents take care of everything for you, bunhead. Like they usually do."

I hated the contemptuous look on his face. He seemed to think I was some spoiled rich kid. "Why don't I start working now?"

"Suit yourself," he said.

Amy held my arm and whispered, "Maybe I can borrow some money from my mom."

I pulled free. "I broke the window. I'll take care of it." I stepped over the sill into the store.

As I left my friends on the sidewalk, I felt like I was leaving the world of light for a world of shadows.

2

The Dragon Palace

Though the window was gone, the air inside the Palace was still warm and damp. I wrinkled my nose at the smell—like old, wet towels. All around me, pumps chuckled and hissed.

In a big tank on the counter were a bunch of little hermit crabs. "Why do they all have different shells?" I asked.

"Because they have soft bodies. When they outgrow their own shells, they have to move into new ones that fit," he said and jerked a thumb behind him at a doorway at the rear of the store. "But you're not here to sightsee. The broom's in the back. You do know what a broom looks like, don't you? A spoiled white girl like you?"

I fool a lot of people who assume I'm white. Though my mom is Chinese, I have the same pale skin, brown hair, and green eyes as my dad.

"My mother's Chinese," I told him.

He said something that I recognized as the Mandarin dialect, which sounds flatter than my own family's Cantonese dialect because it has fewer tones. It also didn't have the final consonants on words that Cantonese had.

When I looked blank, he laughed harshly. "Liar."

"I don't speak that dialect," I said in Cantonese.

His forehead furrowed. "Are you trying to speak Chinese?"

I could feel myself bristling, but I managed to keep control of my temper. He had every right to be cranky. After all, I'd broken his window.

"I am speaking Chinese," I said.

He chuckled. "No, you're speaking Cantonese. That's not Chinese."

Until my grandmother had come to America, I had ignored my Chinese heritage; but, bit by bit, I was putting the pieces together. "There are a lot of dialects in China."

"But only one true dialect," he insisted. Obviously, he thought that was his.

I hadn't run into such snobbishness before from a Chinese. "Most Chinese here speak Cantonese."

He smiled as if he were humoring a child. "Cantonese are not true Chinese, either."

I sucked in my breath. I wished I could have used Chinese, but my vocabulary wasn't up to it. I switched back to English. "I've heard of having a chip on your shoulder, but you've got one the size of a telephone pole."

He rubbed his chin. "I guess I was wrong," he said. "You're not a spoiled white girl."

"No, I'm not." I glared.

He paused as if he had trouble finding an English equivalent for the Mandarin phrase "You're a spoiled half person."

"I'm a full person," I said, balling my hands into fists. I was one word away from hitting him. I could understand his disliking me because he believed I was careless, but I couldn't understand his disliking me for being only half Chinese. I guess racists came in all colors.

I was so mad that for one moment I was ready to stalk out of there and take the consequences for the broken window. However, that would only make him feel he was right. And I like to think that I take after my grandmother, who never takes the easy way out of things. I'd stay long enough to pay for the window and maybe knock some sense into him at the same time.

"I'm a full person, and my name is Robin, Robin Lee," I corrected him. "What's your name?"

"Mr. Tsow," he said slowly, as if he thought I would never remember it.

"I'll get the broom, Mr. Tsow," I said stiffly, and pushed past him. When I went through the doorway he had indicated, I found myself in a room full of metal shelves filled with boxes and cans, pumps and filters. I didn't know there were so many types of fish food.

There were also more tanks full of fish. From what I

could tell, the bulging fish were pregnant, but I was no expert. There were also jars filled with water that were labeled with dates.

Before this, I'd never given much thought to a fish store. It was just someplace you went to when you wanted to get a friend for the goldfish you had won at the school bazaar. I was starting to realize, though, that a fish store was a pretty elaborate setup.

"Are you taking a nap, bunhead?" he called from the front.

"I'm looking," I said, growing frustrated. "Where's the broom you said was here?"

"It's in the corner by the back door," he said. "If you don't recognize it, come back out here, and I'll draw a picture for you."

I wish he'd told me where it was the first time. When I came back out again, he was breaking the last pieces of the glass from the window frame. "There's a trash can behind the counter," he said. "You can put the pieces in it."

I went around behind the counter and found a trash can. It was full of take-out cartons, so I mashed them down with my foot.

He limped behind the counter and dumped the hammer there. "I'm going to get some plywood to cover the window. Watch the store."

"What do I do if a customer comes in?" I asked.

He shrugged. "Tell them to wait." Taking a set of car keys from his pocket, he stepped awkwardly through the window frame. There was something wrong with his left foot.

His car was parked right in front, and there was a paper bag over the meter as if it were broken. He took off the bag and stuffed it into his pocket. Then he climbed into the car and turned on the motor. Black smoke spewed all over from his old clunker. I didn't see how it got past the smog inspections. Some of it drifted through the open window frame, and I wriggled my nose in disgust.

He pulled out into the street and double-parked long enough to take out some orange cones from his trunk and set them in the place where his car had been. Then he took off with a roar, as if he were trying to win a race.

I was determined to do a good job, so I swept the glass together and began filling the can. I reached the top in no time. I was afraid to leave the store alone to search for a bigger can, so I just swept the rest of the glass into a pile.

When he roared back, he put the cones back into his trunk, then he parked and slipped the paper bag over the meter again. So that was how he kept his own parking space. In our neighborhood, the Richmond, cars cruised for parking spots like hungry sharks.

I then thought of his injured left foot and called through the open window space. "Do you need help?"

He untied a rope from a pile of plywood stacked on top of his car. "No."

He wasn't exactly the talkative type.

"What do you want me to do with the glass? The trash can is full," I asked.

Though he was slim, he handled the top sheet of plywood easily. "Put it in the trash, of course."

"But where's the trash?" I asked.

"There's a Dumpster in the back," he said. Though he had plenty of upper body strength, his bad foot made it difficult to balance the sheet of plywood. It swayed from side to side as he staggered toward the storefront.

Despite all of his insults, I felt sorry for him as he limped back to his car. After his awkward effort with the first sheet of plywood, I thought he'd welcome help now. "That really looks like a job for two people," I said as I climbed through the empty window frame.

He whirled around on his good foot in an almost graceful pirouette. "I can manage on my own."

"It'll go faster if I help," I said. As I moved toward him, I bumped into the first board, which was leaning against the storefront.

"Watch out," he said, and sprang from his good foot. It would have been a move any dancer would have envied—except it was done faster than a regular one. Unfortunately, he had to land on his bad foot. He shoved me away as he stumbled.

I had jarred the heavy sheet of plywood so that it had begun to fall. It would have hit me if he hadn't pushed me. His momentum carried him forward into the falling board, slamming it back up against the building.

"Are you all right?" I asked, heading over to him.

He glared at me as he straightened. "Next time just do what I say, bunhead. Or don't you understand English? Do I have to learn Cantonese to give you orders? Or does a half person have just half a brain?"

Cheeks burning, I used the door to reenter the store. I was mad and embarrassed . . . and yet, despite his insults, I was curious, too. I'd seen him leap with all the gracefulness of a dancer. Though he was slender, he'd handled the plywood easily enough, so he must have muscles—also like a dancer.

It was his bad foot that threw off everything—like a bird with a broken wing.

I went back to the trash can, but it was too heavy. No matter how I grunted and strained with my dancer's muscles, I couldn't budge it.

He must have heard me puffing as he stacked a second plywood sheet by the storefront. "What's the matter now?" he demanded.

"The can's too heavy," I said, straightening.

"What kind of help are you?" he asked.

I found myself flushing. "Sorry. I'm a dancer, not a weight lifter."

He clicked his tongue in exasperation. He pulled a slip of paper from his back pocket and began to write furiously. "You can feed the fish, then. Here's a list. You'll find open boxes under the counter."

I was supposed to use a bright yellow package to feed the tanks of small fish. I found it under the counter next to an old radio. It was so old, it had knobs for dialing and for volume. I figured I might as well have music while I did my chores.

It had been tuned to one of those all-talk radio stations, but I turned it quickly to my favorite station. As the first notes drifted through the store, I heard a bang that made me jump.

I looked outside to see that he had dropped a third sheet against the car and was rushing as best he could back to the store.

I gave a jump when he shouted, "Turn that off!"

"I-if you don't like that kind of music, I could find something else," I offered.

His hand chopped at the air for emphasis. "I hate music. Didn't anyone teach you not to touch another person's things?"

I seemed to have a knack for making him madder and madder. "I'm sorry."

He snorted contemptuously. "You must have a lot of practice apologizing. What's wrong with you? Americans and Chinese each respect other people's property. You should have got a double dose of that lesson."

"Okay, okay," I said quickly, trying to calm him. "I'll get your station back."

I couldn't remember the number of the original station, so I had trouble finding it again.

"I said turn it off, bunhead," he snapped.

"Don't be so upset. I'll find it," I said, frantically turning the dial.

He threw a leg through the empty window frame. "I'll get it myself later," he said. "For now, just turn it off."

Hastily I snapped off the radio. "Sorry." And to myself I said, All right. No more mistakes. I'd show him that I had a brain.

"And don't you ever touch my radio again," he said as he got the hammer.

What a grouch. It was going to be really hard to work for him. However, you learn to dance with a lot of aches and hurts. I would manage to put up with a pain like him.

"You must like some kind of music," I coaxed.

He slipped a box of nails from his pocket. He must have bought them when he'd gotten the plywood. "I'm very democratic. All music is a waste of time."

I came around from behind the counter again with the box of fish food. "Everyone likes some kind of music. It's like breathing."

"I'm not just anyone." He studied me and then gave a sharp, harsh laugh. "I knew a dancer back in China who used to think like you."

Curious, I asked, "What happened to her?"

"It was a him," he grunted. "They have male dancers, too, you know."

"Of course they do," I bristled.

He jerked his head at me. "That dancer found out the hard way that dancing was even more of a waste of time than music."

I'd met people who didn't care about ballet before, but

I'd never met anyone who hated dance itself. And it was especially puzzling coming from someone who would have had so much grace if not for his bad foot.

I wish Madame were here to defend ballet, but there was only me, so I had to do my best. "But dancing is just a special expression of what every body does: move. If you have a body, you dance. Ballet just refines it. It's so natural. I mean, it's like hating a sunset."

"Sunsets," he announced earnestly, "are wastes of time, too."

I had never encountered someone so full of hate before. "If you hate beauty, all that's left is ugliness."

He stared at me almost sadly. "You're young yet. When you grow up, you'll see that's being realistic."

I shook my head. "I'll never give up dancing."

"That's what he said, too, when he was your age." He used the claws on the hammer head to scratch his chin. "But like all dancers, he had his brains in his feet. He pounded them so much with dancing that there was nothing left. I'm just trying to save you from his fate."

For once, I was at a loss for words. How can you be nice to someone that lives in such an ugly world?

And Mr. Tsow was just as ugly and as horrible as his world.

It was going to be a long three months.

3

The Real Beast

While he nailed up the plywood, I began to feed the fish.

I was determined to show him that I was a good worker, but as I went from tank to tank, I slowed down to sightsee a bit. I'd never realized just how many different types of fish there were to sell. In fact, I had never given much thought to fish before. I mean living fish. The only fish I liked was steamed and served in a black bean sauce.

As I fed them, I couldn't help watching. Some were tiny silver lightning bolts. Others drifted serenely through the plants like shiny clouds gliding through the forest tops. When I shook the food into the tanks, the fish swarmed upward, tiny mouths working overtime to gulp down the food.

The neon tetras were bright streaks of blue and red. They darted together first one way and then another. It was like seeing a picture of living arrows, zipping to the left and then to the right. Or a corps de ballet of soldiers dancing first one way and then the other across a stage battlefield.

If they'd been dancers in Madame's school, they would have been the energetic beginners running around in ballet slippers—just so happy to be on the stage.

The orange swordtails swam about with long black tails sharp as daggers. I thought of them as intermediate boys trying to be so cool while they danced the battle scene between the soldiers and the mice in *Nutcracker*. I hated rehearsals for that one because it meant dodging their cardboard swords.

I didn't see any piranhas, though, which would have matched Mr. Tsow's personality.

As the plywood went up over the window frame, the store became darker and darker until it felt even more like a cave. The only light was the eerie glow from the tanks.

The banging of the hammer began to echo as the plywood covered the window, growing louder and louder until it boomed. Some of the fish were racing back and forth frantically as if they were getting more and more nervous.

Not the angelfish, though. I think I liked them the best. They had such fine, long feathery fins and tails and their black markings shimmered against their silvery sides. As I watched them swim through the water, I thought of a dancer trailing long ribbons. They moved so smoothly and effortlessly. It was how I wish I could dance.

There was one I especially liked. It had long fins that trailed, and it glided through the water as gracefully as Madame's star pupil, Eveline, across a stage.

Another fish circled around the first one, with fins and gills spread wide. Beauty and the Beast would have danced around each other just as lovingly at the end of their ballet. I could have watched the pair for an hour.

I found myself relaxing as I listened to the gurgling of the pumps and aerators, which sounded like a brook. Pretty soon I could feel the tension in my shoulders ease. I could see why some people kept an aquarium.

When I suddenly heard an oath from outside, I remembered Mr. Tsow and my job.

Guiltily checking the list, I saw that the angelfish had their own special food, so I got it. Gently I dusted it over the surface of the tank. The flecks swirled around in circles to the motion of the pumps. And the angelfish began to get excited, darting around in circles as they nipped at the food floating above.

Suddenly Mr. Tsow shouted, "Not so much!"

I turned to see him in the doorway.

Anxiously he limped over toward me. "The fish will eat until their stomachs burst."

He stopped by the tank of angelfish, his eyebrows drawn together in worry lines, gazing at them almost as if they were his children. The light from the tank cast grotesque shadows over his face. He almost didn't seem human . . . more like a beast.

And yet as his eyes followed the angelfish with the longest fins, his face softened. The fish seemed to sense he was watching because it drifted in a graceful circle, sweeping its long fins behind. "Look at you," he said to the dancing fish. "You're almost ready."

"Ready for what?" I asked.

His face grew harsh when he remembered me. "To have babies," he snapped. "If she survives your care."

He found two small nets with tiny mesh to scoop out the excess food from the fish tanks. "Here. Remove the food from the rest of the tanks before you kill the fish."

He did the angelfish tank himself, cautiously skimming the food flakes from the surface. His face grew even gentler. "Easy, now, easy," he said in a soothing voice. From the TLC, I figured this fish must be one of his favorites.

I went from tank to tank, scooping out the food and dumping it into a plastic bag. When I had finished, I heard him cooing gently to his favorites. "Sa, sa, I won't hurt you, lady." Tenderly he netted the fish with the long fins and lifted her into the air.

"Easy, easy," he reassured her as she flapped frantically within the net. When he eased her into a smaller carrying tank, he shifted the net so it belled outward full of water. With a gentle shake of his wrist, he drew the net smoothly away from the frightened fish.

As the fish swam around anxiously, he spoke soothingly to her until she calmed down. He was just as gentle with her partner.

I suppose if I'd had fins and a tail, he wouldn't have minded if I was only half Chinese. "What would you like me to do next?" I asked.

"Try taking the glass out in batches," he ordered. "There's a large empty box behind the counter."

And if I'd had fins and a tail, I think he would have used his nicer voice. But I was a human and humans didn't count. No, make that half human. So I was even less.

I found the box behind the counter and put some of the glass into it. When I lugged it into the back room, I saw that Mr. Tsow was transferring the pair from the small carrying tank to a larger tank with a piece of slate at the bottom. When I took a better look at the tanks, I saw some of them also had pairs of angelfish. I guess they were going to have babies, too. Other tanks were empty except for a piece of slate covered by a cloud of fine blue threads. When I looked closer beneath the threads, I saw they were covered by tiny little bubbles.

He grunted. "Before you ask, they're eggs." He took a magnifying glass from a shelf and held it out to me. Some of them were milky white, others were covered with fuzz. But in some I thought I saw small dark things moving. When I looked closer, I almost dropped the lens because there were eyes looking back at me.

I set the box of broken glass down with a clink and looked more closely. "Something's wriggling inside the eggs," I said. There must have been four hundred eggs on the slate.

"They'll hatch in a few days," Mr. Tsow explained. "Not all of them. The ones that are white aren't fertilized."

"And the fuzzy ones?" I asked, moving the magnifying glass around.

"That's fungus growing on dead eggs," he said. "But I should get a few hundred at least."

"That's a lot of angelfish," I said, lowering the magnifier.

He indicated some of the other tanks. "I breed a lot of fish, but," he added proudly, "angelfish are my specialty. I've created my own special hybrids. That's what I'm doing with this pair. Their babies will be my own creation. I brought out some of the best features in my other angelfish—longer tails and fins and brighter colors. Hobbyists from around the world buy them."

I turned slowly, looking at all the tanks. "There's a lot more work to a fish store than I'd thought."

He dipped a spoon into a box labeled "Fungus-Go-Way" and added that. "You have to be part biologist, part engineer—and part gambler," he said, lifting his head proudly. "And the tanks always need cleaning."

I peered at another tank. "Water gets dirty?"

"There's fish waste and algae," he explained.

Pointing at one of the jars of water, I asked, "And what's in there?"

"Invisible fish," he said.

I leaned so close that my nose was almost against the glass. "I don't see them."

"I told you they were invisible," he said.

I figured they must be some kind of fish that was so transparent that I couldn't see them in the dim light of the back room. "I hope customers don't pay you with invisible money," I said.

"They wouldn't dare," he said grimly.

I thought of all the tanks in the store. "You mean you have to clean each tank?"

"The fish won't do it for themselves, bunhead," he grunted. "And they won't keep the filters working or the pumps going or set the thermostats just right, either."

I set the magnifying glass down on a shelf. "It's like running your own little world here," I said as I squatted and picked up the box of glass.

"But it's worth it," he said. "Fish are just . . . lovely. Angelfish can't help being anything but beautiful. Unlike people, there's no talk. No politics. All you have to do is feed them and take care of their homes. And angelfish are the best. They're the most energetic and curious. They don't hide like some other fish do. And they're the most graceful, too."

When he put it like that, I could see why he might prefer fish to people. But then he had to add, "And if they don't do what you want, you just flush them down the toilet."

While his words might sound gruff, I realized from his expression that he did not feel that way—especially about his angelic creations. "But I think you'd be sad if you had to do that."

He straightened indignantly. "What makes you think you know so much? You're only a half person. You're neither Chinese nor white, so you're nothing."

Even if I hadn't broken his window, I think he would have been just as mean. I couldn't wait to get away from the Palace.

I'd been right about him the first time. He was a real crab.

No, that was an insult to the hermit crabs.

He was a beast. Thomas could take lessons from him.

4

Homework

I was still upset by Mr. Tsow as I went to my grandmother's. She lived in an apartment that had been
carved out of Uncle Eddy's garage. Like a lot of houses in
San Francisco, the garage was at street level, and the rest
of the house was above it.

I opened the side door to the little alley that ran by the
garbage cans. Uncle Eddy must have been remodeling his
house again because there was a can of paint sitting next
to the garbage cans, ready to be tossed out.

I rang the doorbell, but through the door I could hear
the commotion inside. It sounded like a school play-
ground at recess. When I tried the doorknob, it turned.

Amy's four brothers and sisters were there with Ian.
The collective noise blasted my eardrums and I felt as
though I had stuck my head inside a giant hi-fi speaker.

Calmly sitting in the middle of the storm was my
grandmother. She was hunkered down in front of her

television with a set of game controls in her hands while the kids sat around cheering her on or shouting advice. Amy knelt on the floor, hitting a new ballet shoe against the floor. My grandmother had been shocked when she first saw how we made a new pair of shoes more flexible.

Grandmother's feet, clad in ankle-high, bootlike slippers, were thrust out in front of her. When she had been a small girl back in China, her family had bound her feet, twisting the toes beneath the soles. And now, though her feet were damaged and painful and she needed the help of canes, she insisted on walking.

I shouted, "You really shouldn't leave your door unlocked."

"I do when I have my bodyguards around," she yelled back. She spoke with a slight English accent because she had learned it in Hong Kong, when the British had ruled there. As soon as she had saved the game, she turned around. "Did you have a good practice?"

"I told your grandmother that you had extra practice," Amy said from the side.

"Thanks," I said, flashing her a grateful grin.

"How did you get that cut?" Grandmother pointed at my cheek.

"I . . . uh . . . had an accident," I said—which was the truth.

I got a little nervous as Grandmother examined me. My parents were so busy that I could usually slip things by them—but not my sharp-eyed grandmother. "What sort of accident?" she demanded.

"It was nothing," I answered.

Grandmother looked at me suspiciously. "Well, you should be more careful."

Fortunately Ian distracted her right at that moment. "Let me take over," he said, holding out his hand. "It's my turn next, but Robin's going to make me leave before I can take it."

"Any minute," I agreed. "We still have to get dinner ready. Remember the contract?"

"Yeah, yeah," Ian said. Our parents had made a contract to have at least some meals together—even if we each had to make sacrifices to be there.

The contract was my brainstorm. My parents were such workaholics that they barely had time to speak to each other or Ian or me. If I hadn't insisted, we would hardly ever see them. Since it was getting near tax time, Mom was going frantic at her bookkeeping job, and Dad was always working both at the camera store and at his true love: making documentaries.

Of course, it meant I couldn't miss dinner, either. Most of the time when we were talking and laughing together, I knew it had been a good idea. However, there were some days like today when I would have liked more time for myself. And when it came to video games, Ian could play day and night.

"All right." Grandmother reluctantly surrendered the controls to Ian. "But I was going to double down."

I glanced at the television. Usually Grandmother was beating her bodyguards at the latest action video game from Uncle's store. (I don't think Mom knew just how gory they were.) However, instead of armed warriors and monsters battling one another, I saw playing cards on the screen. Beneath them the words flashed: "Your bet."

"You're gambling," I gasped in shock.

It was Grandmother's turn to squirm. "I'm studying for my trip to Reno. You want me to win lots and lots of money there, don't you?"

I set my fists on my hips and looked down at her. "But you're also contributing to the delinquency of minors," I scolded.

Grandmother was better at alibis than I was. "You've got it all wrong. I'm teaching them mathematics."

"We know all the odds," said Jason, Amy's brother.

"You see. It's educational." Hoping to distract me, Grandmother picked up a plate of cookies from the floor and offered me one. "Would you like a biscuit?"

Since she'd learned her English in Hong Kong, she sometimes used different words. French fries were chips to her. An elevator was a lift.

"No, thanks."

Amy tested the shoe by flexing it between her hands. "I already tried lecturing them. Give up. They're better than an army of lawyers."

Above Amy's head, tutus for my various friends hung on one wall like huge gauzy flowers. Grandmother was a good seamstress, so she made my costumes and had even learned to make tutus—which made me popular with all the other girls in Madame's school who wanted her help, too.

I plopped down beside Amy. "Ten minutes," I warned Ian. I checked my watch. "Starting now."

Ian hunched forward eagerly. I'd seen him take that pose many times when he was about to destroy a video opponent, but this time he was going to skin a blackjack dealer rather than a monster. "I'll make a million in that time," Ian boasted. His thumbs began to fly.

I flung out a hand toward the television. "I don't know what Ian's really learning," I said to Grandmother.

"You'll thank me when he's a billionaire and can fund your ballet company." Grandmother sniffed. She leaned forward to coach him.

Amy lowered her shoe and rested her head against mine. "How did it go?" she whispered out of the side of her mouth.

Where to start about Mr. Tsow? The racist? The music hater? The bag of insults? If I told Amy about the racism, though, I knew she'd speak to Grandmother.

"He's awful," I said in a low voice, "but I can manage."

"He scares me." Amy shivered.

I remembered how he had been with the angelfish. "He can be nice."

Amy gripped my arm. "How? He was such a grouch about the you-know-what."

I shook my head. "The fish are like his children."

Amy's eyes widened. "And that isn't crazy?"

"A little," I confessed.

"You should ask your grandmother for the money," Amy urged.

"Blackjack!" At that moment, Grandmother gave a yelp of triumph as her pupil beat the dealer.

Numbers flashed across the screen as the kids cheered. I heard the sound of coins clinking as the stacks of Ian's winnings filled the screen. Grandmother was punching the air with her fists. If anything, she was even more excited than Ian.

I would have been a beast myself if I had taken her Reno trip away from her. "Look at her. She's so pumped up about going. It's just three months." I promised myself I wouldn't let Mr. Tsow get to me. "I can put up with anything for three months."

"You hope," Amy said.

5

Old Paint

The next day Thomas and I were awful in practice. We weren't Beauty and the Beast: We were Beastly and the Beastlier.

Though we had tried our hardest, we just kept getting everything wrong—from the steps to the interpretation.

Finally Madame clapped loudly. "Stop, stop," she called.

I covered my face with my hands. "Why did I ever take up ballet? I'm terrible."

Thomas groaned. "You're terrible. The audience is going to laugh me off the stage."

"They will if you keep doing this, Thomas," Madame said. I peeked through my fingers as Madame imitated Thomas's strut. "You are a football player showing off his muscles in high school." Madame prowled across the floor. "But the Beast wants to scare people away."

I couldn't help giggling as I lowered my hands. Now

that Madame had called my attention to it, one of my cousins, who played football, really did strut that way.

Thomas glanced at me, hurt, and then back at Madame. "But I don't want to scare Beauty. I like her."

Madame clasped her hands before her face. "But you do not dare show it. Every other human has hurt you. So as much as you like Beauty, you think she will hurt you, too."

Thomas nodded slowly as her advice sank in. "The Beast likes her, but is afraid of her."

Madame smacked her palms together in approval. "Just so." She turned her attention to me next. "And Robin, you cannot be too soft, too tender at the start. You do not love him yet. You hate. You fear. He is the Beast! Not a football player with a bad haircut."

Thomas touched his hair. "I beg your pardon."

Madame raised a hand apologetically. "I speak only metaphorically, of course."

I thought about what Madame had said. "So I hate him because I don't realize he's human yet."

Madame hunched her shoulders as she tried to find the right words. "And yet at the same time you are curious about him. That is the initial attraction."

"Afraid, yet curious," I repeated, and then shook my head. "I'm sorry, Madame. I don't understand."

"We could rent the cartoon," Thomas suggested.

"No, no, no," Madame said. "The only research you need is yourself. The role you dance is like a lens. A lens lets you focus on things, no?" She held up a thumb and forefinger in a circle and peered at us from between her fingers. "So, the role helps you focus on your life now and on your life in the past. Everything that happens to you is part of your dancing."

"I didn't know you were a philosopher, too, Madame," Thomas said with a smile.

"Philosophy, bah!" Madame dismissed it with an airy wave of her hand. "But dancers must exercise their minds as well as their bodies."

Madame's sister gave a cough from behind the piano. When Madame glanced at her, she held up her watch to indicate it was time.

Eveline and the next group were gathering. "Always you get me to talk too much, Thomas," Madame sighed. "So much to do yet. At least think over what I have said."

Eveline, of course, was Sleeping Beauty. She was an advanced student preparing for auditions with the San Francisco Ballet. She was so good that she was a sure thing to enter the company.

I seemed to be headed in the opposite direction. As I got ready for the street, I watched her limber up. She had such a natural line and everything she did was so graceful—a human angelfish. I loved seeing her dance, and normally I would have stayed for her practice, but I had to get to the Palace.

I peeled the adhesive tape from my toes. I'd gotten

hammertoes when I'd temporarily had to give up lessons and had stupidly practiced on the garage floor. The corns that had developed really hurt.

"How are your feet?" Thomas whispered.

Though they ached, I'd grown used to it. "I've had worse," I said. It was time to see the podiatrist and have him cut the corns down. Today, though, I wondered if it was worth the pain and the trouble. "I guess I can always become an accountant like my mom."

Thomas hopped from one foot to the other as he put on his sweatpants. "I can't even do that much. I'm awful at math. I thought I was being tough. How am I going to be tough enough to be the Beast?"

I recalled what Madame had said about our roles being like lenses for our lives. "Remember those guys who made fun of you last week?" I asked as I pulled on my sweats.

Thomas was so funny that he had a lot of friends at school, but there was a certain small bunch that tried to pick on him. He winced at the memory. "That happens to any boy who wears tights."

"But what did you do?" I prompted.

"Just walked away," Thomas said.

I patted his arm reassuringly. "That was the smart thing to do. But inside, didn't you want to hit them?"

"Yes," Thomas said quietly.

"So maybe the Beast is someone who isn't smart," I suggested. "Maybe all he knows is to hit back."

"Someone who out-toughs the toughs." Thomas

looked thoughtful. "But then he meets Beauty, who isn't a muscle-bound jerk."

I nodded. "So he suddenly doesn't know what to do."

"I'd like to work on this at Leah's," Thomas suggested eagerly.

Leah was the envy of most of the dancers because she actually had her own small practice room in her house. I would have loved to have gone there instead of to that awful dark cave and face the real-life Beast instead of the make-believe one.

"Got to pay off the window," I sighed as I began to unpin my hair. "If you were a nice guy, you'd go in my place."

Thomas grinned. "Not a chance. I'm not the one who keeps losing control of my temper."

"Scum," I said, shaking my hair loose.

"Lead foot." He laughed.

I ducked into the girls' rest room to brush out my hair. For the first time in my life, Mr. Tsow had made me self-conscious about it. When I began taking ballet with Amy and Leah, we had worn our hair up all the time. We didn't know how to do it ourselves, so our mothers had to do it for us every morning.

Even when we had learned how to do it, we some-times wore our hair up all day because it was easier. It was almost a badge of honor. Though I was still proud of being a dancer, I didn't want to give Mr. Tsow any am-munition for his usual insults.

When I got to the Dragon Palace, I was surprised to see the plywood still over the window.

Mr. Tsow had a stupid talk show blasting from behind the counter while he was working on some large, tall jars.

In the dimness, I saw him hold up something between his fingers. "My radio is now safe from you. I took the knob off the radio dial, so don't even think of trying to change the station."

Fine. If he hated music, that was his loss.

I hunted for a safe topic. "How are the babies?"

"Good. Their eyes are growing larger," he said, and nodded toward the back proudly. "Go see, bunhead."

I guess it didn't matter how I wore my hair. I would be a bunhead to him from now on.

When I entered the back room, I saw the couple from the other day still circling in a stately dance. Getting the magnifying glass, I went over to the other tank where I had seen the eggs. When I held the magnifier close to the tank, though, I almost jumped back. The eyes staring back at me were huge.

When I went back outside, I asked, "When will they hatch?"

"Some will be out tomorrow. And they'll all be swimming the day after that," he said as he went on fussing with his jars.

I stowed my bag behind the counter and asked him, "What are you doing?"

"Making brine shrimp," he said.

"To sell?"

"To feed the baby angelfish," he said. He was filling the empty jar with the water from the jar of invisible fish.

"Won't the invisible fish eat them?" I asked.

He rolled his eyes. "A bunhead will believe anything, won't she? What you saw in the jar was just water. There's chlorine in the tap water. You have to let it sit for a few days before you can use it, or you'll kill the more delicate fish."

He worked with all the concentration of a chemist mixing a dangerous explosive. Apparently some fish had to have the water just right. It not only had to be the right temperature, but the right type of water. Some fish liked their water a little acidic, while others liked it more alkaline. I could see what he meant about being part engineer.

"Why hasn't the glass been replaced?" I asked, pointing at the plywood.

Mr. Tsow shrugged. "The insurance company is being slow." He glared at the plywood. "I wish the windows of those insurance people were broken, too. I bet they wouldn't stay boarded up for long."

I remembered the can of paint I'd seen at my grandmother's the day before. "I'll be back."

"You're supposed to start now," he said, glancing at his watch. "Or can't bunheads tell time?"

I was not going to let him make me angry. "You can start the time clock when I return."

He glared at me. "Did anyone ever tell you what a pest you are?"

I thought of my little brother. "Often."

"Well, you don't seem to be taking it to heart," he grumbled.

I went over to Grandmother's. There was the usual noise coming from inside her apartment, so she was already baby-sitting—or, rather, teaching mathematics. Suddenly I heard a loud groan. Someone must have lost their shirt. I hoped that would make Grandmother more cautious about Reno.

I snuck past the door to the trash cans. The paint can was still there. I picked it up to read the label. It was aquamarine. Perfect. I grabbed the handle and lugged it back to the store.

Mr. Tsow was fussing with the filter of one of the tanks. He glared when he saw the paint can. "What's that for?"

"For the window," I explained.

"Well, well, a bunhead with a conscience. Now I can die because I've seen everything." He limped over to me and snatched it from my hands to inspect it. "This is indoor paint. It won't hold up to the elements. If you're going to paint it, you should use outdoor paint."

"Why does it matter?" I demanded. "The insurance company should replace the glass before the paint begins to peel."

He inspected me as critically as Grandmother when she was picking out a sweet orange from a fruit stand. "Dancers think they're so smart. My friend thought he had all the clever responses, just like you do."

Somehow he knew just how to get under my skin. I might have told him off, but right then I remembered what Madame has just said to Thomas: Every experience was part of preparation. Had Beauty hated the Beast this much at first?

I told myself to think of him as research for my role as Beauty, and that helped calm me down a little. "I don't have all the answers. If I did, I wouldn't have a pesky little brother."

"Just remember," he warned me. "There are some situations that are so cruel, they are beyond even your cleverness."

If I hadn't know better, I would have said he was a little worried about me. "Unh, thanks for the advice."

He weighed the can in his hand. "I think there's an old brush in the back."

He disappeared inside and returned with a brush whose bristles curled together like a comma. "The brush will straighten out once you begin painting." He handed me an apron. "Better use this. A girl as clumsy as you will get more paint on herself than the window."

I gritted my teeth. Only three more months of his zingers. "Thanks."

I don't think he was aware of just how much he irritated people. "And don't get paint on the sidewalk."

He got a screwdriver and a newspaper from behind the counter and picked up the can. "Okay, Miss Rembrandt. Let's go."

Once we were outside, I spread out the newspaper while he used the screwdriver blade to pry up the lid. "This blue paint is uglier than raw plywood."

I defended my choice. "It's aquamarine."

"Just because they call it aquamarine doesn't make it aquatic," he snapped.

"Well, it's all the free paint I could find," I snapped in return. Turning my back on him, I put on the apron. "At least the plywood won't look so ugly."

I expected him to go back inside, but to my exasperation, he stood in the doorway to supervise. "No, no, no. Always paint from the top," he said, holding an invisible brush high over his head.

"I can't reach," I said, going on pointe.

His eyes narrowed. "I thought even bunheads were smart enough not to go on pointe on concrete."

Before I could ask him how he knew that, he disappeared inside.

Coming back out with a stool, he banged the legs onto the sidewalk. "Step on this."

I was so surprised at his thoughtfulness that I stammered, "Th-thank you."

"Just don't try to get out of work by breaking your neck, Miss Prima Bunhead." He had to turn a kindness into an insult.

I was getting used to his typical beastly behavior, so the insults didn't bother me as much. As I climbed carefully on top of the stool, I asked, "Was it your friend who gave you all these wrong ideas about dancers?"

He leaned toward me like a prosecuting attorney. "Why do you want to be a dancer?"

I had to take a moment to think. "Because when it goes right, it's the closest thing to flying. And the audience is flying with you."

He gave a start, and then his face got a faraway look. "What did I say wrong now?" I asked.

His mouth turned down sadly as he shook his head. "My friend thought just like you did, but then he found out the hard way that dancers always come back down to the earth. And although the audience claps for you while you're in the air, what they really want is to have you on the ground where they can pelt you with garbage."

Stunned, I lowered the brush and stared. I had never met anyone who wanted to see things through dark glasses all the time. He didn't just hate dancers and ballet and half Chinese. He hated everyone. He was an equal opportunity bigot. "People aren't like that," I insisted.

He made a disgusted sound at the back of his throat. "Now you look like you're going to cry. I really am trying to save you from a painful lesson, bunhead. People like being stupid and ugly. And they hate anyone who's special or who makes them feel special."

With his lips curled up scornfully, his face almost

looked like a mask—the kind of mask the real Beast would have worn if he had wanted to wear a disguise.

And, yet, in his eyes I saw something else . . . worry.

And I remembered what Madame had told Thomas about the make-believe Beast. Inside the ugly creature was a human being after all. I'd seen it when he brought out the stool. And I was viewing it now.

"But not everyone's like that," I tried to assure him.

His mask didn't change, but his eyes . . . I'd never seen such sadness before.

I must have stared at him too long, because he turned away abruptly.

"You'll just have to learn the hard way," he grunted as he limped back inside.

Someone had put the worry in his voice. And someone had put the sorrow, too. But when and how?

I wondered if the imaginary Beauty had been just as curious about her Beast.

6

A Little Decorating

All the way home, I kept wondering about Mr. Tsow. I still didn't like him, and I hated the idea that I would be stuck in his store for so long.

Even so, I couldn't help thinking about what had made him the way he was. For the first time, I began to understand what Madame had meant in her comments to me.

I had been running around the floor in pure terror—like some victim trying to escape a monster in a horror movie. Madame had told me that you can sometimes feel two different emotions—feelings that might move in opposite directions.

So, though Beauty wanted to flee the Beast, she was also just as curious about the creature as I was about Mr. Tsow.

That night, as I practiced in the living room, I tried to put both feelings into my dancing. At a certain point in the steps, I was supposed to move away on pointe and end in an arabesque. And then I was supposed to hold that position while the Beast danced.

I hadn't thought about why I didn't keep running, but stopped dead in my tracks. Now, though, I pretended as if my own curiosity were halting me in mid-flight. And when I finished off my arabesque, I stared at the Beast. I tried a few different expressions, but finally I tried to act like I was a bird gazing at a snake: afraid and yet fascinated.

It felt right, but I'd see what Madame said.

The next day at rehearsals, I thought I must have been crazy to figure I could interpret the role myself. Thomas, though, seemed to be doing fine. He must have taken Madame's instructions to heart, because she wasn't making those funny little faces whenever he danced.

I wish I could have said the same for me. I felt like I was out of control on the practice floor. Finally I stopped. "Please, Madame. I'm slipping and sliding all over. I need more rosin."

Thomas ran his foot over the floor. "I think it's sticky enough already from the rosin on everyone else's shoes."

"I'd just feel better," I said miserably. Walking over to the box of rock rosin in the corner, I ran my shoes through it for a better grip. However, I knew the problem wasn't a slippery floor. It was me.

The worst moment came when Thomas was supposed

to get close to me for the first time. I was supposed to shove him away. I wound up hitting Thomas so hard that he gave a grunt and stumbled; but like a real trouper, he kept on dancing.

From the corner of my eye, I could see Madame scribbling furiously. I almost lost my nerve, but I thought if I was going to get scolded, I might as well go for the gold-plate lecture. So when I had moved away from Thomas and did my arabesque, I looked over my shoulder as I had last night. I pretended I was wondering about Mr. Tsow.

To my satisfaction, Madame murmured, "Good."

That was high praise from Madame, but I got so carried away that I stopped being careful. Thomas had been right. Enough rosin had come off on the floor to make sticky spots and I felt a sudden pain in my calf.

When she saw me wince, Madame stopped the practice. "You are all right, Robin?"

Bending over, I massaged my calf. "It's just a little strain. I'll be fine tomorrow."

Thomas ran his hand over the floor. "It feels like someone poured glue over here. Your shoe probably got stuck."

Madame knelt, feeling my leg, and then rose with a grunt. "I think we will stop for today." She turned to her sister. "We clean the floors tonight."

Madame must have also thought we had improved because she didn't repeat her old notes. "Good, Thomas. I see you fear and pretend to be strong."

"I'm sorry I was so wild," I said to Madame, then I turned to Thomas. "And I didn't mean to hit you."

Thomas rubbed his chest. "I'm used to it."

Madame patted me on the shoulder. "Do not worry about being wild. We practice to put things into balance. Today I see you fear and hate. And then . . ." She imitated my stare at Thomas. "The interest." She gave me her notes—lots of them—but she finished with an encouraging smile. "This was a good practice. You must work more, of course. And keep that leg warm, Robin."

"Yes, Madame," I said, relieved that we had finally done something right. I made my reverence—though it was a bit awkward because of the muscle pull.

When we had left, Thomas nudged me. "Maybe you ought to go home and soak that leg in warm water. I'll do your job at the fish store."

I couldn't expose Thomas to Mr. Tsow's tantrums, too. Who knew how he would insult another dancer? After all, it had been my bag that broke the window. "I ought to be able to work off the muscle pull on the walk there." And I started off.

Thomas looked worried. "You're limping pretty badly."

I fought to walk more normally. "See. It's already going away."

However, as soon as I was out of Thomas's sight, I let myself limp again.

I was sure the injury would make me a target for Mr. Tsow's sniping so, even more than usual, I hated having to see him. Since he was going to insult me anyway, I didn't bother putting my hair down. Today I was a bunhead and proud of it.

The Palace, though, was so changed that at first I didn't recognize it. It was only when I got to the corner that I realized I had passed it.

Instead of the half-painted plywood, I was looking at a palace under the sea. Jellyfish floated like large pink flowers. A dragon peeked over battlements and mermaids played tag in a garden of coral.

It was the fish, though, that were the wonder. I saw all the fish from the shop and some I didn't recognize. Some had fins like long silken veils. Others had so many spines that they looked like fireworks.

And in the center was a dragon with long, flowing angelfish fins. It seemed to be flying rather than swimming.

When I opened the door, the loud chatter from an all-talk radio station hit my ears.

"What happened?" I asked loudly.

Mr. Tsow was busy doing some kind of chemical test on a tank. "I was going to ask the same question. You're on time."

However, he couldn't put me off with rudeness today. I jerked my head toward the plywood. "I mean the window."

He shrugged as if he was embarrassed. "It bothered me, so I did something about it." He made a point of ignoring me as he made a note on a pad. "Hmm, the pH is down."

I was flabbergasted. It was like finding a pearl in a dumpy oyster. I would never have guessed that a sullen lump like him could have that kind of talent.

"But it's good enough to be in a museum," I said as I shuffled down the aisle on my gimpy leg.

He reminded me of an older Chinese, like Ah Wing, who never wanted to take a compliment. "It's a good thing you don't buy paintings for museums then, or they'd be filled with junk. I'd never have doodled on the window if I'd known you were going to carry on this way." He turned to go on scolding me, but stopped when he noticed my odd gait. "What happened to you, anyway?"

"I pulled a muscle," I said and gritted my teeth for the zinger that was sure to come.

Instead, he tapped his notepad against his fingers. "Then go home. You won't be of any use to me that way."

I wasn't going to postpone my freedom any longer than I had to. "It's not like I have to lift crates, just boxes of fish food."

My defiance infuriated Mr. Tsow. He flung his notepad at me angrily. Fortunately, he was a better painter than he was a pitcher and missed me by several yards. "I told you to get out!"

Though I was scared, I unslung my bag from my shoulder and dropped it on the floor. After all, I was the granddaughter of a crippled woman who had walked across China with three small children. "Look. You don't like me. And I don't like you. So let's not prolong the agony one day more. I want to work off my debt as quickly as I can."

He rubbed the back of his neck agitatedly. "But you could hurt yourself worse."

I forced myself to be calm as I picked up his notebook. "I know you don't think much of bunheads. And even less of half people." I grabbed his hand and slapped the notebook on his palm. "But if I make a mistake, I pay for it."

Embarrassed, he flipped the notebook back and forth over his fingertips. "I might have been wrong."

"About bunheads?" I asked.

"No, bunheads will always be bunheads." He gave a little cough. "But I might have been a little wrong about half people."

Suddenly I felt good. Half of an apology was more than I had ever expected from him.

Before I could thank him, the door opened and a woman and a little girl came inside.

The little girl paused at the top of an aisle, turning slowly as she drank everything in with wide eyes. She took in a deep breath of the damp air and then exhaled in delight. She signed to the woman.

"My daughter," the mother translated, "says that your store is like magic."

The little girl must have come from some pretty miserable hole if she thought this dump was magical.

"My daughter would like a pet," the woman said. "Could you recommend something?"

I expected him to snap her head off, but Mr. Tsow just stood there.

"Excuse me," the woman said uncomfortably. "Do you speak English?"

Mr. Tsow managed to get control of himself. "Yes. Is this her first pet fish?"

The little girl must have been able to read lips, because she signed without waiting for her mother to translate.

"It's her first pet anything," the mother explained.

Mr. Tsow actually smiled. I nearly knocked over the tank of hermit crabs because I didn't think his face had those muscles.

"Well, then," he said, "let's make sure we get a sturdy one for you."

The little girl looked hopeful as she made more signs.

"And pretty?" her mother asked.

"And pretty," he agreed.

I don't know what magic the little girl had, but it sure was working. With great patience, he began to show them the fish.

Almost immediately the little girl came to a dead stop by a tank of rainbowlike fish. The little girl said through her mother, "Those fish are so beautiful. But why are they separate?"

The tank had glass partitions dividing it into little rooms. In each room was a solitary fish.

"They're Siamese fighting fish," Mr. Tsow explained to

her, and then glanced over his shoulder at me. "Better watch out, bunhead. They're also dance critics."

The little girl pointed at more tanks. Every one of them had a story. Some fish came from the Amazon River in Brazil. Others came from Africa.

The little girl signed again to her mother.

"It's like a United Nations of fish," her mother interpreted.

"Except my fish are better behaved," Mr. Tsow said. I think he enjoyed showing off for such an appreciative audience.

Suddenly I began to see things through the little girl's eyes. I don't know why I'd thought of the Palace as an ugly cave. It was really like a grotto under the sea, and the fish were living jewels glowing in the dark. I now saw what the little girl had seen when she'd first come through the door. The Palace really was magical.

Finally she stopped before some neon tetras. The little girl jabbed her finger enthusiastically at them.

"Well, those would need a heater," Mr. Tsow said, glancing at the mother.

She shook her head slightly at the extra cost.

Mr. Tsow squatted down so he was eye-level with the little girl. "Hmm," he said, studying her until she shrank back against her mother. Finally he gave a nod as if deciding she were worthy enough. "I've been saving Harold for someone special like you."

The little girl glanced up at her mother and signed something.

"Who's Harold?" her mother asked for her.

"My special friend. We talk a lot," Mr. Tsow said.

As sales pitches went, it was too corny even for the little girl. She signed skeptically. "Fish don't talk."

Mr. Tsow scratched his head as if hurt and puzzled. I could only guess at the superhuman effort it took for him to be nice to someone. "Of course fish don't talk. But you don't need words to tell people things."

"No," the little girl said cautiously through her mother.

"You tell me things with your hands," Mr. Tsow said.

The little girl got annoyed and signed furiously. Blushing, the mother raised an index finger to the little girl in warning. Then she gave a little cough. "My daughter says that fish don't know sign language, either. And they don't have hands."

The little girl glared at Mr. Tsow. I don't think she liked to be patronized.

Mr. Tsow hastily explained, "But you use more than your hands to talk to someone. You use your face and your body." He paused and then added, "Like dancers."

I gave a start because that's the way I felt about ballet. I guess it must have been another tip from his mysterious friend.

The little girl, though, still looked doubtful. "Fish don't dance," the little girl insisted.

"At least meet Harold," Mr. Tsow coaxed.

The little girl clung to her mother as we followed her

over to a tank of goldfish. Mr. Tsow pointed at a white fish with orange markings. "There, you see that fellow?" Harold swung obligingly in a wide circle so that his long tail and fins trailed like ribbons. "He's saying hello."

The little girl pressed closer to the tank and signed to him.

"My daughter's greeting him," the mother said.

When Harold answered by spiraling away, the little girl crowed in delight. She signed to Harold.

"She's inviting Harold to our apartment," the mother explained. She glanced at the price of the goldfish and looked relieved.

With the same tenderness he showed all of his fish, Mr. Tsow patiently angled the net until he had snagged Harold and put him inside a plastic bag for the little girl. "Do you need a tank?"

The mother shook her head regretfully. "I think we'll make do with a kitchen bowl."

"But you won't be able to see Harold that well." Mr. Tsow went over to a stack of fish bowls. "I've got one I was going to mark down. See, it has a little chip."

If there was a chip, it was so small, I couldn't see it, but the mother and little girl seemed happy enough. As if I hadn't had enough surprises, he threw in a small box of fish food for free.

When they had left, he glanced at me. "What are you staring at?"

"You," I said. "Why were you so nice to them?"

He leaned over and rose with the box of food in his hand. "It must be a full moon."

If anyone was a Beast, it was Mr. Tsow. And yet through his brush he could take you to a dragon's palace. And he could be kind to a small girl. And he knew about the heart of dancing: Artists use paints and a dancer uses her body.

"For someone who hates dancing, you know a lot about it," I said.

He shrugged, returning to his old irritable self. "Anything I know I learned through my friend."

Wanting to be helpful, I held out my hands for the box. "Here, that's my job."

He turned awkwardly so that his body shielded the box from me. "I said go home."

I tried to reach around him. "I can't until I do my work."

He stumbled back awkwardly. "Why do you have to be so stubborn?" he complained in exasperation. "I told you. Those injuries can get worse if you don't take care of them."

"How do you know? Your friend again?"

He set the box high on a shelf where it would be difficult for me to reach. "I read it in some magazine. Besides, you're clumsy enough with two legs. I can only guess at the damage you'll do with one leg in these narrow aisles. We'll count today as a day's work. Satisfied?"

Amazed at his generosity, I asked, "Why?"

He shrugged uncomfortably. "I told you. It's a full moon."

Now that I wasn't walking or dancing, my leg had started to stiffen up. So I was just as glad he had repeated the offer.

"Okay," I said. "And thanks."

As I limped toward my bag, though, he called, "Wait." I turned to see he had been watching me. "Come with me."

I followed him into the back room, where I checked the tank of angelfish eggs. A cloud of tiny silvery dots now swirled frantically behind the glass. There was no sign of elegant fins or tails as yet. "The babies hatched!"

"Yes," he said as he hunted among the shelves.

I couldn't help chuckling. "They look like a class of beginners. It's hard to believe they'll grow up into beautiful adults."

"I'm sure people have said that about you. Ah, here it is." He held out a small jar with Chinese words on it. "This is a jar of herbal ointment. Rub it on your leg. It'll feel hot, but that's the medicine working."

I was so startled that I just stared at him. He started turning red. Taking my hand, he forced the jar into it.

I finally remembered my manners. "Th-thank you."

However, he was already turning his back on me. "I was going to throw it out anyway."

He said things like that to cover up his kindnesses. Real beasts don't decorate windows or give away goldfish bowls. And real beasts don't worry about bunheads who injure their legs.

I remembered what Madame had said to Thomas about the fictional Beast: how he was trying to scare away people before they could hurt him.

Maybe the real-life Beast was even closer to the make-believe one than I had thought.

7

Grandmother's Antennae

Unfortunately, I couldn't rest right away because I had to pick up Ian.

Grandmother was practicing for Reno as usual. Ian and Jason, Amy's little brother, were cheering her on, but Amy's other sisters and brother—Mimi, Didi, and Andy—were playing cards. I was relieved to see it was old maid and not blackjack.

Grandmother looked over her shoulder when I came in. "Amy just called from Leah's. She should be by any moment."

I felt a pang. She had probably been doing additional practice at Leah's. Why did I have to break that window? "Great," I said as I limped over toward the sofa.

Grandmother glanced at my bad leg. "What's wrong?"

"I just pulled a muscle," I said, dumping my bag on the floor.

She studied me a little longer and then held up the controls. "Would you like to play?"

"But it's my turn," Ian protested.

"You said your thumbs were getting tired. Let your sister go." Then Grandmother gave Ian a certain look, and he knew better than to protest.

"That's okay," I said. "I don't want to take Ian's turn."

Grandmother used her free hand to pat the rug. "No, sit down."

I knew better than to argue. "All right," I agreed, "but just one game."

Ian and Jason scooted over to make room for me. Shuffling over, I sat down clumsily beside Grandmother and took the controls from her.

Grandmother leaned sideways to give me a friendly bump. "Now, if you have any questions, don't be afraid to ask."

I can't say my mind was on the game. I kept thinking and puzzling over the contradictions in my Beast. He could be a nice man. Why did he make such a point of acting so mean most of the time?

Ian let out a groan. "You had twenty. Why'd you take another card?"

Jason pounded a fist on the floor. "You just went bust."

Grandmother studied me thoughtfully. "You're as wizard as your mother at math."

"Sorry," I said. "I guess my mind is someplace else."

"Yeah, Saturn," Jason said.

Grandmother pried the controls from my hands. "Why don't you boys take over. Robin, I need to take some more measurements for your costume."

"I thought you had all the measurements you needed," I said.

"I need more," Grandmother insisted.

"We can play on without you," Ian said.

"Yes, just save my points," Grandmother said. She had amassed over ten thousand dollars in the game.

I let out a whistle as I got up awkwardly. "You're going to clean up in Reno."

Grandmother shuffled over to her sewing table while I trailed her. Grandmother was a proud woman. Because she didn't want anyone feeling sorry for her, Mother, my uncles, and I were the only ones who knew she had bound feet, and she had made us swear never to tell anyone else.

Supporting herself on one cane, she opened a drawer. Inside were stacks of different tins and jars. Only half the labels were in English, and though, with Grandmother's help, I could speak Chinese, I couldn't read many words.

Before Grandmother had joined us in America, I didn't pay much attention to Chinese things. Back in those days, China had been the Great Wall and nothing else. Since she had been with us, though, I had begun to realize just how little I knew. There were so many small, everyday things that made up her Chinese world that I didn't know anything about. Her apartment was like a window into another universe—one that I was just beginning to explore with her help.

She tapped a finger against her lips as she surveyed the drawer.

"Now, where was my tape measure? Oh, here," she said, taking out the long cloth strip. All the numbers were in Chinese. "Now do you want to tell me what's up?"

I positioned myself near the table. It had to be a certain spot so Grandmother could support herself against the table while she used her two hands to measure.

"Nothing," I said.

Grandmother set her canes against the table and then leaned on it. "Then where were you?" Grandmother demanded. "There's a big recital coming up. I would have thought you would have been at Leah's practicing with Amy, injury or no injury."

Mom had once warned me that Grandmother had even better antennae than she did when it came to sensing things. Grandmother could have picked up trouble on Mars.

As I raised my arms, I thought about lying and saying that I had been studying for a test at the library, but I couldn't fib.

"Before I tell you," I said, "you have to promise to go ahead with your trip to Reno."

Grandmother wound the tape around me. "Why?"

"Because you've been having so much fun planning on this trip"—I held my hands in the air—"and I'm counting on you to pay for a ballet production."

Grandmother jotted down some notes on a scrap of paper. "What has your problem got to do with my trip to Reno?"

I rested my hands on my head. "Very little, but that's what you have to promise."

Grandmother began to measure again. "I can't make that kind of promise," she said.

I tilted my head so I could see her face better. "It's just that I don't want to complicate your life even more."

Grandmother looked hurt rather than angry. "You don't think I'll understand because I'm so ancient."

I wanted to hug her, but I had to stand still. "That's not it at all," I said hastily. "You're one of the youngest people I know."

"Then why can't you tell me?" she asked sadly.

"Okay," I sighed, "but you have to at least promise not to tell my parents."

"Well, it's probably nothing that I can't handle," Grandmother said confidently.

Which is exactly what I hadn't wanted. However, when her grandchildren were in trouble, you could no more keep Grandmother out of it than a fish out of water.

"I sort of took an after-school job." I told her about the broken window and the job at the Dragon Palace. "It's just for three months, so please don't tell my parents."

Grandmother frowned. "Robin, what you did could have been dangerous. You should never have taken a job with a stranger without consulting me or your parents, first."

"My friends knew," I said. That was a lame excuse, and I realized it even before Grandmother raised her eyebrows. "I won't do it again," I added. "Are you going to tell my mother?"

Grandmother twisted the measure around her fingers. "I really ought to."

"Please don't," I begged. "She'll ground me for sure, and then I'll miss the recital."

"You should have thought of that before you threw your bag." Grandmother unwound the measuring tape. "There are other ways to get revenge on a boy. And I know them all. You just come to me."

For Ah Wing's sake, I hoped he stayed on her good side. "Next time, I will. Do you have to talk to my mother?"

Grandmother stood there for a moment, watching the tape swing back and forth as if it were a set of scales tipping first one way and then the other. "The problem with your mother is that she overreacts," Grandmother said slowly and then sighed. "So I guess I won't. But why didn't you come to me for the money?" Right then someone must have won big-time, because we could both hear the clinking of video coins over the cheering. She answered her own question. "Oh, you wanted me to go to Reno."

"You and Ah Wing are so excited," I said.

"Reno will always be there," Grandmother said. "You're more important." She slung the tape around her neck. "I will have to inspect him myself."

I grabbed her wrist. "Oh, please don't do that."

Grandmother was instantly suspicious. "What's wrong?"

"He's not a bad man—though he can be rude and insulting," I said, letting go. "He said I was a . . . a half person."

Grandmother whipped the tape from her shoulders. "He did! Well, I'll set him straight." Grandmother held the tape measure in both hands as if she were ready to strangle anyone who insulted her grandchild.

I tried to head off any mayhem. "But he apologized," I said hastily.

"He'd better," Grandmother said, flexing the tape threateningly.

"Do . . ." I hesitated, then asked softly, "Do other Chinese think that about me?"

The tape snapped taut between her fingers. "Who else said that?" Grandmother demanded.

"No one else," I said, "but maybe they're just not telling me to my face."

Grandmother used the back of her hand to caress my cheek. "I won't lie to you. There may be a few who think that. But they're idiots. Anyone who knows you can see how special you are. But don't change the subject. Has Mr. Tsow been treating you right?"

"He can be a beast, but I'm beginning to realize that his bark is worse than his bite. And he can do nice things sometimes. I don't know why he can't be nicer more of the time."

Grandmother positioned me again for measuring. "There are all sorts of beasts in the world. A few are born beasts, and they'll never change. But most beasts are made—either by us or by themselves or by both."

I held my arms out straight as she measured first one and then the other. "Well," I said, "I can see how the world could make some people into beasts—like the kids that get beaten or worse. But how does someone make themself into a beast?"

"Because for some reason they think of themselves as beasts," Grandmother explained. "Maybe they've been told they're ugly all their lives."

"Like the Ugly Duckling," I said, "who was ugly to ducks, but not to swans."

"Precisely," Grandmother said. "So if people have made you think you're a monster, then you act like one."

"How do you convince someone they're not a beast? Whenever he does something nice, and I try to compliment him, he turns nasty again."

"Beasts are afraid of showing they are weak," Grandmother explained.

I thought about how he had reacted about the window painting and about my dancing. Those were signs of weakness, too. "If I could show him that he isn't being weak, but being strong . . ."

"He might start to be less of a beast," Grandmother agreed.

"Thanks," I said.

Grandmother put her tape measure away. "That's what grandmothers are for," she said.

I should have known Grandmother wouldn't stop with just advice. She had warned me.

8

Gone Fishing

By Friday morning, my leg had healed—whether it was Mr. Tsow's ointment or the long soaks in the tub, I don't know. At practice, I made sure to wear leg warmers to keep the muscles warm and loose.

Things went well this time. Thomas and I still had a lot of work to do, but we actually managed to run through the whole piece once without stopping. And we even seemed to be playing our characters better.

Of course, Madame had more notes. The first was on technique and could be handled easily. "We are only working in demi-points shoes now, but I can already see you are forgetting your training. I see you trying to shove and yank your bodies. But you must push downward. Remember what David Howard says: 'A dancer must feel the energy flow through her body in a circle.' " Madame often quoted him.

However, her final note was a kicker. "But you still

dance like you are Robin and Thomas on a date. But you are not you. You are Beauty and the Beast. What is their story really about?"

Inside I groaned. I had enough to think about with the dancing, let alone this, but I didn't dare complain to Madame.

When she saw our blank faces, Madame held her hands out wide. "So I give you a clue. The story is long," she said as she brought her hands together in illustration, "but the ballet piece is short. It is com . . . com . . ."

"Compacted?" Thomas suggested.

I tried, "Compressed?"

Madame nodded her head. "Thank you. Just so, compacted and compressed. And yet in that short time you must tell the whole story to the audience. What happens after Beauty meets the Beast in the tale?"

"She gets lonely for her family and visits them. But they get her to stay too long and the Beast starts pining away."

Thomas patted his hand against his chest mockingly. "His heart breaks and all that stuff. I guess the warranty must have run out."

Madame rapped Thomas on the forehead with her knuckle. "Always the joker, Thomas. Next time I will cast you as a court jester."

Thomas rubbed the sore spot. "I'd be good at that."

Madame folded her arms. "Without a doubt. But I know you can be more." She leaned forward urgently.

"You have talent, Thomas, but you are afraid to use all of it. That is why you play the fool."

Thomas's cheeks grew a bright red, and he shifted his feet uncomfortably. "I think you're mistaken, Madame."

Madame lifted her head in challenge. "I do not know English so well, but I know dance. Thomas, it is time to stop being the village idiot. You will listen or else."

She didn't specify what the "else" would be.

Thomas wisely gave up trying to argue with Madame. Not even Leah tried to do that.

"Yes, Madame," he said meekly.

I tried to come to Thomas's rescue. "So they both fall in love."

"But we must compact-press the whole story into a short dance. You have done the first part well." Madame clasped her hands together. "I see you, Thomas, tough but afraid. Now we must see you trust Beauty. We see you open—like the flower." She spread her fingers outward like petals and then turned to me. "It will come the first time you lift Robin." She turned to me. "And what do you feel when he touches you, Robin?"

"Well, I'm still afraid, yet curious," I said.

"And?" Madame coaxed.

I thought about it a moment. "But then when I'm up in the air, I might like it."

Madame clapped her hands together. "Just so. We try."

We ran through it one more time. I was trembling when Thomas lifted me—partly because I wasn't sure if he would drop me. It went okay, though. And when he set me down again, a lot of things seemed to flow naturally because now we both trusted one another.

I would have liked to have run through it several more times, but by then, Amy had come in to rehearse Tom Thumb. The beginners, who would play flowers and toys and such, were chatting excitedly.

"I'm not sure that I see everything Madame's talking about," Thomas muttered as he waved to Amy.

I began to take off my shoes. "But you got the story."

"No, I meant the things she said about my dancing." Thomas shrugged.

I looked up from unzipping my bag. "Can't you take a compliment, Thomas? You really do have talent."

As usual, Thomas tried to turn everything into a joke. "Are you sure you didn't pull a muscle in your brain, too?"

"I wish you'd be serious for once in your life," I grumbled.

"Now you sound like Madame." He chuckled. "I'll leave the worrywarting in your capable hands."

I left rehearsal feeling pretty good—sure that we could take things to the next step now—so I was humming when I entered the Dragon Palace. Mr. Tsow was in the back room fussing with the angelfish newlyweds. "Sa, sa," he was saying soothingly to them. "I'll have you better in no time."

He must have heard me, because his face and voice became stern again. "How's your leg today?"

"I went back to practice," I said. "Can I help?"

"Not unless you can work miracles," he said, worried. "This female fish is sick."

I knew she was one of his favorites. "I'm sorry."

"I've got other medicines besides ointments," he said, holding up a small dark brown jar.

So he was the Palace doctor as well.

Leaving my bag in the corner, I checked the tank holding the babies. The little silver arrows were still as frenetic as ever. Then in the sink I noticed a container labeled BLOODWORMS. I stared at them in horrified fascination. "Do people actually buy these things for pets?" I asked.

"They're the larva of the midge fly," he said, carefully dropping amber liquid into the sick-fish tank with an eyedropper. "I give angelfish parents a special menu— bloodworms are the first course. The second is brine shrimp and finely powdered food flakes."

"Yuck," I said.

"They'd probably say the same thing if they saw you eating a hamburger," he grunted. "By the way, what sort of exercises do you do before you dance?"

"The usual ones," I said cautiously. I thought he might be setting me up for another one of his zingers.

He cleared his throat nervously. "That friend of mine, the dancer, used to do tai chi in the morning as well."

I figured he was making that up. But I couldn't say why. "I don't know tai chi."

He hesitated a moment and then muttered, "I know a little. Enough for a beginner."

It took me a moment to realize he was offering to teach me. Even then, I didn't believe my ears. "You'd show me?"

He shrugged. "The Chinese have been doing it for a couple of thousand years. Maybe they know something about how to keep even a bunhead's body limber."

I blinked. Why was he offering to do that? He had been kind in many small ways, but teaching tai chi would require much more effort on his part. "I don't want to put you to any trouble."

"I just thought you might want to learn something about your culture," he sniffed.

I realized he had said "your" culture. So he must consider me Chinese now. That was a big step for someone who had considered me only half human when we'd met.

I was so grateful that I almost gave in. But did I really want to learn from him? He'd probably make tai chi like some kind of boot camp. "I don't know if I have that much time."

He scratched his cheek. "We could include it as part of your hour."

My jaw dropped open. Why was he being so generous?

It made me think again about what Madame had said about the Beast. Inside, Mr. Tsow had a kind heart, I thought, but someone must have hurt and scared him just as badly as the Beast had been.

For a moment I almost accepted his proposal. But who would be my teacher—the tenderhearted Mr. Tsow or the Beast?

So, as tempting as the offer was, I shook my head. "Aren't you busy with the store?"

He sucked in his breath as if I had just hit him in the stomach, but all he said was, "You're right. It doesn't make much sense, does it?" He turned back to his fish.

I felt bad. After all, he had been trying to reach out to me, and I had rejected him.

I was still trying to figure out what to do when the door suddenly opened and Grandmother shuffled into Mr. Tsow's lair. I stopped dead when I saw her. She had warned me that she was going to check him out, but I hadn't expected it so soon.

Ignoring me, she stumped over to the counter. "I'd like a fish," she announced loudly.

Mr. Tsow looked up from the thermometer he was using to check a tank's temperature. "Well, there'd be a problem if you wanted a cactus."

The tenderness from the day before seemed to be gone, and the Beast was back firmly in control.

I hurried over. "Can I help you?" I asked in a loud voice and then whispered, "Why aren't you baby-sitting?"

"I sent them off with Ah Wing to a movie. I told you I was going to see where you work, and I've been wanting a pet," Grandmother whispered back. In a loud voice, she said, "No. I want something with personality."

"If you want cute, try a puppy," Mr. Tsow snapped as he made adjustments to a heater. However, if he thought he could insult my grandmother, he had picked on the wrong person.

Lifting one of her canes, she used it to poke his side. When he finally faced her, I thought I saw her give a little start. She certainly gazed at him long and hard. I guess she was trying to decide for herself if he really was a bad man.

Angrily he shoved her cane away. "What are you staring at?"

"Nothing," Grandmother said, setting the tip of the cane back on the floor. "And I don't want cute, I want something with teeth." She clicked her own together in illustration.

I thought Mr. Tsow would get mad, and I got ready for the battle of the century, because no one pushed Grandmother around. However, he leaned his head back and actually smiled. "When a pet has teeth, you can get hurt if you get careless," he warned.

Grandmother stamped one of her canes. "Do you think I would have lived this long if I was careless?"

It was the first time I had ever heard Mr. Tsow laugh. "You're a regular tiger, aren't you? Well, I guess you're tough enough to handle a piranha, but we don't stock those."

Grandmother tilted her head back. "So what do you have?" she demanded.

"How about some angelfish?" Mr. Tsow suggested. "If it helps any, they're cannibalistic."

"Then they'll remind me of the landlords I've had back in Hong Kong," Grandmother said. She watched him carefully again.

"I wouldn't know," Mr. Tsow said. Tucking the testing thermometer into his shirt pocket, he put his hand on a shelf for support as he shifted his feet. "I'm from Beijing myself."

"But lots of northern Chinese visit Hong Kong," Grandmother said. I thought she was trying to make conversation.

"One place is a lot like another," he said as he limped from around the counter.

He kept to a pace that made it easy for Grandmother to follow him down the aisle. "San Francisco is so very different from Hong Kong. It can't be the same as Beijing, either."

Mr. Tsow turned sideways to glance at her. "The scenery may have changed, but the people are just as foolish."

I was trailing Grandmother, so I leaned forward to whisper, "See what I mean about him?"

She only nodded as she followed him over to the tank of angelfish. "These are my favorites," he confessed.

Grandmother gazed at them. "They're beautiful."

He watched them as well, his eyes shifting from side to side as they followed the fish. His voice and face changed as he gazed at his angelfish. "I don't think there's any fish quite as graceful."

I couldn't help asking, "Like dancers?"

"Please," he said, making a face. "Unlike bunheads, angelfish know what they want: food and a nice clean home. No tantrums. No fancy airs. And they never get tired. Every movement of an angelfish is lovely."

Grandmother had taken her eyes off the tank and had focused on him, studying him intently while he spoke.

"There's no backbiting," Mr. Tsow went on. "They'll fight, but they're honest about it. You know it's over territory."

Mr. Tsow went on listing the virtues of the angelfish. When he was done, Grandmother asked, "You care a lot about your fish, don't you?"

He straightened and turned in a slow circle as he looked around his kingdom. "I'd just as soon fry and eat them," he said in perfectly Beastly fashion.

Grandmother shook her head. "You don't find out all that information about something that you're just going to eat. You learn that for something you love."

"I have to have fish to sell." He shrugged. "And fish aren't machines that you can just stick batteries into to make them run. You have to take care of them just right."

Grandmother glanced at the tank of his special angelfish. "Why do these cost so much more than the others?"

"They're lovely, for one thing," Mr. Tsow sniffed.

Grandmother peered at them and then nodded her

head slowly. "Well, they do look like they're worth the price."

"And I bred them myself for those features," Mr. Tsow boasted. "So they're unique."

"Well, I'm sold," Grandmother said. "Do you deliver? I don't live far from here."

When other customers had asked him that, I had heard him tell them no and call them lazy—he'd especially seemed to enjoy refusing. However, he glanced at Grandmother's feet and then at her canes. "Normally I don't, but I guess your hands are full."

Grandmother seemed to be able to bring out his human side rather than the Beastly one. Maybe he sympathized with her because of his own limp.

"I don't want to have to strap the fish to my back," Grandmother explained with a laugh. "I could get wet. And it's not my bath night."

He laughed again and then waved a hand at me. "I guess I could leave long enough while my assistant is here."

So I'd been promoted from clumsy idiot to assistant now. I wondered if that went with a hike in salary, too.

Grandmother pretended to notice me for the first time. "I'm sure she's very helpful."

Mr. Tsow just laughed. "She's a bigger help to the insurance companies than to me."

No one picked on her granddaughter while she was around. As Grandmother turned slightly, she rapped him accidentally across the shin of his good leg with a cane. "Oh, I'm terribly sorry."

Mr. Tsow limped again out of range of her canes. "That's all right. I still have another leg."

Grandmother beamed at me. "I'm an excellent judge of character. You'll bless the day you hired her."

Mr. Tsow opened his mouth as if he were going to zing me again—but thought better of it even though he was beyond Grandmother's reach.

Of course, there was also a tank to buy and then a heater and a filter and a pump. And sand to go in the bottom, and plants as well. By the time he'd totaled it up, I began to worry about her Reno fund.

I sidled up to her and whispered in her ear, "Don't you want to think about this?"

"No, I've been wanting a pet," she whispered back. "And one that I don't have to take for a walk."

"But that's less money for Reno," I pointed out.

"I'll win it back," she said smugly, and added, "but you'll have to feed them while I'm gone."

When Grandmother had paid for everything, Mr. Tsow got a small plastic bag and net and they went back to the tank. "So which one do you want?" he asked her.

Grandmother studied the tank and then shifted her right cane over to her left hand so that she could hold two canes in one hand. With her free hand she pointed. "That one."

"That's the best one in there," Mr. Tsow said. He

sounded almost sad to let it go. "Are you sure you don't want a different one?"

"The others just aren't right." Grandmother's finger followed her choice. "No, it has to be this one."

Mr. Tsow raised the lid. Setting an empty bag inside the water, he reluctantly guided her new pet into the floating bag. As he tied up the bag, he acted as if he were selling his own baby.

While he was gone, I started to clean the trash from the little can in back of the counter. At the bottom of the can, I found his studies for the window. In the swirls of circles and lines, I saw rough sketches of a dragon—and not just stiff, static creatures, but dragons flying and swirling. They had fins that were as long and fine as ribbons—like angelfish.

They were crude things, and yet I couldn't bring myself to throw them away. When the insurance company replaced the plywood with glass, the painting would be lost. At least this much would survive. Folding the sketches up carefully, I stowed them in my bag.

Since it was only a few blocks to Grandmother's, I expected Mr. Tsow back soon. So I was surprised as the time went on and he still hadn't returned. We had a couple of customers, but fortunately they paid in cash. I didn't know how to handle credit cards or checks.

My hour was nearly up when Mr. Tsow finally limped back inside the Palace.

"I was afraid you weren't coming back," I said.

"She's a long-winded old auntie." He shrugged. "If she hadn't run out of chocolate biscuits, I would still be there."

I was sure that my cunning grandmother had bought those biscuits just so she could grill him.

9

Foxy Grandmother

After work, I made a beeline for Grandmother's. She was holding a small can of fish food at an angle over the tank, near her television and video game set. "Trust you to work for *the* Mr. Tsow."

I paused mid-charge. "What do you mean?" I asked puzzled.

She gave the can just one tap. Mr. Tsow had already trained her not to overfeed the fish. "You didn't recognize him?"

My mind leaped to the most obvious conclusion. "Is he some kind of murderer?" I thought Grandmother might have seen his picture on one of those real-crime shows.

Grandmother laughed as she watched the flakes of food swirl around on top of the water. "No, he's a famous ballet dancer."

My jaw dropped in amazement. "Him? That's impossible."

Grandmother set the can down near the tank. "I don't remember the exact year, but it was something like forty years ago. The National Ballet of China came to Hong Kong as part of an Asian tour. He was their principal dancer."

Now I knew how a computer felt when it was getting overloaded with strange information. "You saw him dance?" I asked.

She fiddled with the pump until the ribbon of bubbles rose faster through the water. "No, but his picture was all over the Hong Kong newspapers and magazines. He was quite handsome. Quite a few girls had crushes on him." She gave a snort. "Quite a few women, too. Some of them should have known better."

I wrinkled my forehead. "You're sure?"

Grandmother got her other cane, which was leaning against the television set. "My feet may be crippled, but my eyes and mind are just fine," she snapped in annoy-ance.

"Of course," I said quickly as I followed her over to the sofa. "It's just that . . . well, it's hard to believe. He hates ballet now."

As Grandmother sat down, it was her turn to be amazed. "Really? But he was so famous for it."

I plopped down next to her. "Well, do you know what gave him that limp?" I asked.

Grandmother shook her head. "No. But I've been reading a little bit about the ballet now that I have a ballerina in the family. It worries me sometimes. It worries your mother, too. Dancers always have to face the risk of an injury."

"You heard the mean, spiteful things he says about ballet now. And especially dancers."

Grandmother studied the tank. Bubbles from the aerator ran in a silvery ribbon to the surface, twisting and turning as if dancing. "He likes you. Maybe he's trying to save you from what happened to him."

I had to laugh. "He doesn't like me."

Grandmother turned and put her arm around me. "Maybe he sees a little of himself in you."

I remembered that other day. "He had said I had reminded him of a dancer he knew."

"It was himself," Grandmother said confidently.

"Me?" I asked in a small voice. "But I'm just an intermediate."

"He must see the same spark in you that he once had," Grandmother said.

I didn't think that was true. If he saw anything in me, it was a sign of how desperate and lonely he was—feelings that I don't think he admitted even to himself.

I leaned my head against Grandmother's shoulder. It seemed made for being my pillow. What had happened to Mr. Tsow? And what had turned him against dancing itself?

Try as I could, I couldn't imagine anything that would make me hate ballet. Dance was dance. What happened to dancers didn't change Dance itself.

"I'll always find some way to be part of ballet," I swore, "even if it means sweeping the stage."

One of Grandmother's canes clunked against the floor as she put an arm around me and hugged me fiercely. "When you're young, that's the way you love something."

"I love you that way," I said.

Her hand stroked my hair. "I loved your mother and uncles just the same way."

I heard the sadness in her voice. "What's wrong, Grandmother?"

She kissed the top of my head. "Nothing."

And suddenly I realized what it was. "But even though you loved that much, you had to let them go," I said, raising my head.

Grandmother lifted her arm away. "That's the other side of love. America was better for them than staying with me in Hong Kong. But losing them only made me miss them all the more. However, other people react in a different way to a loss."

I leaned forward to pick up one cane. "Such as?"

Grandmother took it and rested it with her other cane, where she could reach them easily. "Sometimes when you lose something you treasure, the love turns to hate."

"How can you hate something you used to love?" I asked.

"If you want a lot of fancy-sounding reasons, you should call one of those radio psychologists." Grandmother shrugged. "But I think you try to convince yourself that you don't need it anymore. And you give the hate the same passion that you did to the love."

"If you can't have it, then you don't want it," I said slowly. "He even hates all kinds of music now. He'll only listen to all-talk radio shows."

"That tells you how great his pain is," Grandmother said.

"That's awful," I said. I felt so sad as I turned to watch the angelfish in the tank. The fish was still trying to adjust to its new surroundings. It twisted and turned frantically as if it were in a trap, yet as desperate as it appeared, it moved with lovely grace.

Grandmother put her arm around me. "It's not your fault."

As I watched Grandmother's fish, I realized that Mr. Tsow had not turned his back completely on dancing. The angelfish were as close as a fish could come to a dancer, and the angelfish were Mr. Tsow's favorite.

And that thought just made me so sad: a crippled dancer hiding in a dark cave of a store watching his graceful fish.

So his ballet friend was all a lie. He knew about dance because had been a dancer himself. His tai chi offer had been genuine. And I had cut him off.

That made me feel even worse. He had finally tried to reach out to someone. And I had refused him. How deep a hurt had I done?

"I've just got to know what happened to Mr. Tsow," I swore.

"I don't think he'll tell you if you ask him," Grandmother admitted.

I put my arm around hers. "If I don't find out, I'll explode."

Grandmother winked. "The nosiness must run in our family. We'll be partners." I think she enjoyed sharing secrets with me.

The door burst open that moment and children flooded into the room. Amy's family and Ian charged together toward the television set.

"Hey, you got a fish," Ian said. Right away he had to tap on the tank.

"Don't do that. You're scaring it," I said as the fish began whirling around in tight circles.

Jason had been just about to knock on the glass himself. "So we shouldn't?"

"Of course you shouldn't," Grandmother said. "Now turn on a game."

An exhausted Ah Wing finally appeared in the doorway. "I'm worn out. How do you do it?"

"I'm not old like you," Grandmother teased.

Ah Wing slumped against the door frame. "I'm too tired to argue."

I got up so he could sit next to Grandmother. "Do you want something cold to drink?"

He pressed a fist against his stomach. "I had a soda the size of a trash can," he said as he burped.

"And popcorn," said Andy. "The big, big tub that you can refill as many times as you want." He held up the huge basketlike tub that he was carrying. They must have refilled it before they had left the theater, because it was full of popcorn, scenting the air with the smell of artificial butter.

"And candy," Mimi said, shaking a box of Junior Mints.

Grandmother frowned. "You've spoiled their appetites for dinner."

Ah Wing sank down beside her. "And mine." Closing his eyes, he leaned his head against the back of the sofa. "Now excuse me while I take a nap. I earned it."

"Not yet," Grandmother said, poking him. "Do you know a Tsow? He runs the fish store over on Geary."

Ah Wing sighed wearily. "A fish store? Has he got any flounder fillets? I love them in black bean sauce."

"Not that kind of fish," Grandmother said, giving him another nudge. "He sells pet fish. Like that."

Ah Wing opened his eyes and followed her pointing finger to the tank. "You bought a fish from him? Is he your new boyfriend?"

"I don't have an old one, yet," Grandmother said. "Now answer my question."

Ah Wing sat up straight. "Tsow . . . Tsow, can't say that I know him."

"He'd be from the Mainland," Grandmother said.

"So he speaks with a northern accent," I added. "And he has a limp."

Ah Wing shrugged. "Nope, that doesn't ring a bell, either."

"Well, tomorrow we're going to find out," Grandmother said.

"But Saturday's my day off," Ah Wing protested.

"It will do you good to meet people," Grandmother said.

"If it isn't driving you around to garage sales, then it's this," Ah Wing grumbled. "All right. Where are we going?"

"Get to bed early. First thing in the morning, we're going to the coffee shops and ask around," Grandmother instructed him.

Though she had only been in America a short time, she'd already developed her own granny network of news and gossip in Chinatown.

"That could take all day," Ah Wing groaned.

Ignoring his complaints, she turned to me. "Can you come, Robin?"

I felt frustrated. "I won't be free until sometime in the afternoon. It's our first full rehearsal, and I can't say what time it'll finish. Sometimes they go on a long time."

Grandmother planned our strategy like a general. "Then Ah Wing and I will do the garage sales in the morning. And in the afternoon the three of us will go around the Richmond and get some answers. We can meet you here."

"What can you find out in this neighborhood?"

Grandmother looked at me as if I had just gotten off the jet from Hong Kong. "We don't need to go to Chinatown for the latest gossip. The gossip has come out here."

"They don't call the Richmond the second China-town for nothing," Ah Wing said.

The trouble was, could I wait until tomorrow to find out more about my Beast?

I glanced at the angelfish. The noise was only making it more frantic. I could have headed over to Leah's and maybe practiced. But I just had to know what had happened to make Mr. Tsow into a Beast.

"Could you drop Ian off at home?" I asked. "I'd like to go to the library."

Ah Wing gave me a thumbs-up. "Good girl. Studies are important."

Grandmother knew just what I was "studying."

"You go ahead," she said.

I didn't have any luck at the local library. They only kept the newspapers for a month. The microfilms of old newspapers were at the Main Library, but the librarian said they were mostly the San Francisco papers. The only out-of-town one was *The New York Times*.

She guided me over to a series of fat books called the *Readers' Guide to Periodical Literature*. She said they listed articles in magazines—though, again, I'd have to go down to the Main Library for them as well. However, I couldn't find anything about Mr. Tsow. Though there were a lot of articles on ballet, they were on America and Europe, not Asia.

If there was anyone who knew everything about ballet, it would be Madame. It was near dinnertime when I got to the school. The door was locked, but the lights were on inside, so I knocked on the plate glass.

A moment later I saw Madame come out of her office. In her hand was a half-eaten piroshki. That was a Russian fried meat pastry.

When Madame saw me, she walked to the door and unlocked it. "What is it, Robin? Did you forget something?"

I did a quick little reverence. "I'm sorry to bother you, Madame. But I was wondering if you had ever heard of a Chinese dancer named Tsow."

"Which ballet company is he with?" Madame took another bite of her piroshki.

"He danced with the National Ballet of China some thirty years ago," I said.

Madame chewed thoughtfully and then swallowed. "Yes! I remember him. If he'd entered the dance competitions, he could have taken the top prizes. He was wonderful. His technique was perfect. Very precise."

"You saw him here?" I asked eagerly.

"No, in those days, it was the Cold War. I don't think America had recognized Mainland China yet, so he couldn't have come over. I was still in Europe when his company came through on tour." Madame lifted her piroshki like a champagne glass. "I have not thought of him in many years. He was the toast of the Continent at one time."

"A Chinese dancer?" I asked in amazement.

"In those days, the Chinese ballet dancers studied the classical Russian style," Madame said. By Russian, she meant the best. "And today the Asian dancers win all sorts of prizes. But he was one of the pioneers."

I made a note to find out more about them. However, in the meantime I couldn't help thinking of that bitter old man. "Then what happened to him?" I asked.

Madame shook her head. "I don't know. One moment he was shooting across the sky like a rocket. And poof." She spread the fingers of her free hand like an explosion. "He was gone. It's a terrible shame. He was . . . superb."

Mr. Tsow must have been good. Madame didn't praise people easily.

I thanked her and let her get back to her meal.

So one answer just led to more questions. I felt like I was opening up one of those Russian dolls where you keep finding smaller and smaller ones. I'd have to wait until I could check the auntie-grandmother network. That was better than any library if you wanted the truth.

10

The Stumblebums

Saturday was our first attempt at a full rehearsal.

Madame had marked out an outline of the stage in masking tape. Even though we had all practiced individually, it was different trying to put it all together in a group. We got in one another's way on and off the "stage." Sometimes things got so jammed that it looked like gridlock.

Madame had to keep untangling us all morning. It made me wonder how this chaos would ever become a recital.

Thomas and I were feeling pretty good about our own piece after yesterday's practice. However, it was as if there were some stumblebug infecting everyone. We were tripping all over the place. And when we weren't falling, we were stepping on one another. I felt like the rankest beginner. No, we were worse, because even the beginners were laughing at us by the end.

We were so bad that Thomas stopped making his lit-tle wisecracks. When rehearsal was finished, Madame asked us to stay.

Miserable, we got into our sweats and waited while Madame gave the rest of the company their notes.

"It'll be okay," Amy whispered to me as she left.

Leah just squeezed my hand.

Thomas hung his head. "Go on. Say it. I stunk."

Normally Leah likes to zing Thomas, but that's only because Thomas is usually so good. Today, however, she just patted him on the shoulder.

"Forget it," she said sympathetically.

I shook my head. "It wasn't your fault. You're a great dancer. So it has to be me."

"You're almost as good as Eveline," Thomas insisted. "I'm sorry for letting you down."

That was a lie, but I appreciated his fibbing like that. "Well, when you're down at the bottom, you can't get any worse. Only better."

"That's what you think," Thomas said. "I bet I'm going to set a new low."

The studio felt awfully empty when everyone else had gone, even Madame's sister.

Glancing at us, Madame consulted her notes and then beckoned.

She cleared her throat. "What happened?"

I couldn't look her in the eyes. "I don't know, Madame. But we'll work extra hard."

"You already work hard," Madame said. "But maybe I gave you too many notes on your characters yesterday. Today you were thinking so much that you forgot the dance."

"Is that why we stumbled around?" Thomas asked. "And I thought it was just because we were clumsy."

Madame did not bother with a lecture this time. She just arched her eyebrows eloquently.

Thomas knew the signs by now. "Sorry, Madame," he said, and lowered his head to provide a more convenient target for the rap of the knuckle.

As Thomas rubbed the sore spot and Madame massaged her finger, she said, "So we make it simpler. Forget about romance. All the notes on your characters come down to one thing: What does each really mean to the other?"

"A hernia?" Thomas quipped. Another rap of the enforcing knuckle. "Ow!"

"I ask another way. What is most beautiful in your own lives?"

"Dancing," I said without hesitation.

Thomas swallowed, afraid of the notion. "Ditto."

Madame slapped us both on the shoulders. "So think about what it is to lose dancing and then find it again. Monday we begin fresh at the next practice."

"Yes, Madame," I said, making my sign of reverence.

Despite Madame's encouraging words, we were both feeling pretty depressed as we headed for our bags.

I slunk all the way over to Grandmother's apartment. I was not only failing at ballet, but also at solving the mystery of Mr. Tsow.

When I got to her place, I could hear video game noises from inside. I knew it couldn't be Ian because he was with Dad at the latest Wolf Warrior movie. "Is Amy's family here?" I asked when Grandmother answered the door.

Grandmother put a finger to her lips for me to be quiet. "No, but we're doing research."

"Ai-yah!" a man shouted.

"Mind your manners," Grandmother called quickly. "Robin's here."

Usually a cheerful person, Ah Wing scowled at the television set. "This game's fixed," he snarled, setting down the game controls. "The dealer's made blackjack ten times in a row."

"Don't be silly. A microchip can't cheat," Grandmother said.

Ah Wing put a hand to the side of his mouth and leaned toward me confidentially. "Personally, I think it hates to lose."

"So the 'research' isn't going well?" I asked.

Grandmother pointed at the screen. "I'm doing fine." She had nearly twenty thousand in her account now. Ah Wing, however, was going to go bankrupt soon. So Thomas and I weren't the only ones flunking out today.

"Maybe you should stick to slot machines," I suggested to Ah Wing.

"But there's no battle of wits," Ah Wing grumbled.

"Precisely," Grandmother teased.

After discussing Ah Wing's best strategy for bank-rupting Reno, I got to ask Grandmother about what she had learned about Mr. Tsow.

"Not much," Grandmother confessed.

I told her what Madame had told me last night. Then I used her shower and changed into a dress I had brought.

When I came out, Ah Wing patted his stomach. "I know what's thrown off my game. I'm hungry and that's distracting me. I was just thinking a snack would help me concentrate better."

"Let's start at Sweets," Grandmother said. "Auntie April will be there. She knows everything."

"I've never heard of that," I said. "Are you sure that's in the Richmond?"

"Of course," Grandmother said, getting her canes. "You've just ignored it because it's where old-timers like to hang out."

Grabbing his cap from the sofa, Ah Wing jammed it on his head. "Come on now. Gossip is like extra cream on my cake."

11

The Sweets

Ah Wing drove us over to Clement Street in his taxi.

Clement Street was a mixture of Asian stores, delis, and restaurants—not just Chinese, but Vietnamese, Japanese, Thai, and Indonesian as well. By now the street was filled with mouthwatering aromas, but Ah Wing stopped his taxi in front of a little coffee shop.

It's funny, but I walked Clement almost every day and had never noticed it before.

Through the window, I could see cheap plastic chairs in front of small formica tables. Around them sat elderly Chinese men and women nursing Styrofoam cups—I assumed they were filled with tea or coffee.

"Just like in Chinatown," Grandmother said with a wave of her hand.

As usual, Clement was one long traffic jam of cars, so Ah Wing let us out, and I escorted Grandmother inside while he hunted for parking.

When we came through the door, the customers called out their greetings. Apparently Grandmother was a regular here.

"Try the strawberry cake," a woman customer called. "Only three people got sick on that today."

Grandmother nodded and smiled, but said, "I feel like chocolate today."

At the back of the coffee shop was a counter filled with small slices of cake and pastries. The woman behind the counter greeted Grandmother politely.

"Let's see. A slice of chocolate cake for me and strawberry cake for Ah Wing," Grandmother said. "What would you like?"

I hadn't heard Ah Wing make any selection in the car. "Don't you want to wait for Ah Wing to make his choice?" I asked.

"I'm going to have some of his anyway, so I might as well pick out something I like," Grandmother said.

I picked out a chocolate chip cookie. Then I carried the little paper plates over to a vacant table.

The lady who had recommended the strawberry cake leaned over from her table. "So you took the chocolate." She clicked her tongue in disapproval. "And you used to be so smart. You shouldn't hang around Ah Wing so much."

Grandmother studied the two slices. "Ah Wing's slices are always so much bigger. This way I can take some of his without feeling guilty."

As they chatted, I filled Styrofoam cups with tea from a big urn.

"This is my granddaughter, Robin," Grandmother said proudly when I brought the tea over. "She's a ballerina."

The woman scanned me like radar. I thought it was because I didn't look Chinese, like my mother, but like my father. "How do you do?" I asked politely in Chinese.

I saw from her eyes that I had gone up a notch, but I still didn't quite pass inspection. "You're too thin."

By now I was used to Grandmother's friends, so I just smiled. "The cookie will help."

"You should eat cake. Lots of it," she urged. "Children should look prosperous." Several other women nodded their heads as well. From their prosperous shapes, they obviously followed her advice.

"She has to be thin," Grandmother defended me. "Someone has to lift her into the air." Then she turned to me. "This is Auntie April."

While Auntie April pretended to pat my hand, her fingers pinched my skin lightly. I think she was checking on how much flesh was really there. "You eat here a little more often and maybe I'll introduce you to my grandson. He has baseball cards worth a hundred dollars each."

"Imagine," Grandmother gasped.

Auntie April sat back. "Who would think cardboard would be worth more than gold?"

"I still put my trust in gold," another woman said. She held up her wrist to clink her bracelet.

"You shouldn't wear that outside, Granny Ding," Auntie April scolded her. "Too many punks around."

A third woman mentioned a friend who had been robbed. "They knocked her down and stole her bracelet right in broad daylight. Broke her arm, too."

That touched off a round of crime stories that circled around the coffee shop. It actually got a little scary and depressing. However, no matter what crime someone described, Auntie April always knew someone who had it worse. The funny thing was that she was almost cheerful about all the misery.

All this time, I was squirming inside, wanting to learn more about my Beast. I knew Grandmother would have to chat with her friends first. If it had been Dad or my American friends, I would have gotten right to the point. From my visits to Chinatown with Ah Wing and Grandmother, though, I knew that would be rude.

When Ah Wing finally walked in, they were covering some crime that had happened ten years ago when a clerk had gotten shot in a candy store up the block.

"Try the strawberry," Grandmother said.

I noticed that Grandmother had not only eaten her chocolate cake, but Ah Wing's as well. All that was left were reddish smears.

"I was feeling like chocolate, though," Ah Wing said, eyeing the counter.

"The strawberry is better, isn't it, Robin?" Grandmother gave me a warning look.

I knew that expression too well to argue. "Yes, it is."

"Well, if Robin says so," Ah Wing said.

"We have tea for you," I said, though when I felt the sides, it was lukewarm.

Grandmother nudged me. "You watch. The lady behind the counter will give him a huge slice."

Auntie April rolled her eyes and teased Grandmother. "That's because she likes him. Better watch out."

Grandmother gave a snort. "She just feels sorry for him."

When Ah Wing set his plate down, Grandmother pointed at the cake. "See. Look at the size of those strawberries."

"You can have some," Ah Wing sighed. It seemed to be an old argument between the two of them.

There was a new round of teasing and gossip before Grandmother got around to asking, "Do you know that man that runs the fish store, the Dragon Palace? I bought a fish there the other day."

Auntie April shook her head. "He's a northerner. What would I know about him?"

"Why would that make any difference?" I asked.

Auntie April laughed and waved her hand around. "We're all from southern China, or our ancestors were. We speak the Cantonese dialect, while that man speaks the Mandarin." She curled her lip slightly as if that were a major flaw of Mr. Tsow's.

I remembered Mr. Tsow's own comments about southerners. "Why don't northerners and southerners get along? We're all Chinese."

"But the northerners have had the capital for four thousand years," Auntie April said.

With a forkful of Ah Wing's strawberry cake on its way to her mouth, Grandmother interrupted her. "Except when the Mongols took the north." Grandmother knew more Chinese history than anyone else.

Auntie April shrugged. "I think the northerners like to forget about that. And anyway the northerners think they're purer Chinese than us, so they don't like to have much to do with southerners."

"It's like strawberry and chocolate cake," Ah Wing explained, "and they're arguing over which is more cakey than the other." From his wistful glance at the chocolate cake on the counter, I knew where his heart lay.

12

The Taipei Gardens

When we were outside once again, I asked, "Where do we go next?"

"And this time I'll pick out my own cake," Ah Wing said.

"I know what's wrong," Grandmother said. "To find out about a northerner, you have to ask a northerner."

"What northern Chinese do you know?" Ah Wing asked.

"Nobody, but I know a busybody who has a foot in both communities," Grandmother said. "Let's find a pay phone."

We found one on the corner. "Change," Grandmother said, holding out her hand. She looked as serious as a surgeon asking for her scalpel.

Ah Wing fished a dime and a quarter out of his pocket and Grandmother handed me the coins. "Call your friend Amy."

"Amy's southern Chinese, too," I said as I dropped the coins in.

"But her mother has a friend, Auntie Ruby, who knows everyone, even northerners." Grandmother smiled.

"Who's Auntie Ruby?" I asked.

"She was an amah to one of the richest families in Hong Kong," Grandmother said as she leaned on her canes. "She was practically another grandmother to their kids."

"Did you know her there?" Ah Wing asked.

"No, I met her here. I was having lunch with Amy's mother." Since they had both come from Hong Kong and Grandmother sometimes baby-sat her children, she and Amy's mother had become good friends.

"But what has she got to do with northern Chinese?" I asked as I began to punch in the number on the keypad.

"Since she came here, she's become a kind of one-woman employment agency for amahs," Grandmother said. "Rich northern Chinese families have been coming to her, too."

I still didn't quite see the connection. "But if she's just an employment agency, how would she know about the northern Chinese?"

Grandmother chuckled. "Maybe I didn't put it right the first time. She thinks of herself still as an amah, but she's now an amah to all the San Francisco Chinese. That means she does more than find jobs. She dabbles in just about everything—matchmaking and peacemaking between feuding neighbors."

"But how does she make a living at it?" I wondered as the phone rang.

Grandmother shifted from one cane to the other. She could be as restless as Ian. "It's Chinese style. She does a favor for you so you do a favor for her. And somehow it all works."

Ah Wing nodded. "If she was back in China in a little village, she'd be a fixer."

"Oh," I said, even though I wasn't sure what they meant.

I straightened a little as someone picked up the receiver on the other line. "Amy?"

"No, this is Stephanie," a girl said. Stephanie Sinclair was the daughter of the man who employed Mrs. Chin. She and Amy were good friends. She must have recognized my voice because she asked, "Is that you, Robin? Do you want to speak to Amy? She's right here."

"Yes, thanks," I said. When Amy came on the next moment, I asked her for Auntie Ruby's number.

She gave it to me and then said, "But Auntie Ruby's treating my mother to lunch right now at the Taipei Gardens."

I turned to Grandmother and Ah Wing and relayed the information.

"That's just a block away," Ah Wing said.

"Thanks," I said. "We'll go there."

"Stay away from Auntie Ruby," Amy added as a warning.

"Is Auntie Ruby some kind of monster?" I asked.

"Worse. She's a fixer," Amy said, echoing Ah Wing. I could hear the shiver in her voice.

When I hung up, I saw both Grandmother and Ah Wing frowning. "What about Auntie Ruby?" Grandmother demanded.

"She's treating Mrs. Chin to lunch," I said, and told her the address.

"Oh, man, she's toast," Ah Wing groaned.

"What's so awful about Auntie Ruby?" I asked.

"There's no such thing as a free lunch with Auntie Ruby," Ah Wing said. "Maybe we'd better wait."

Grandmother, though, wanted to know about Mr. Tsow as much as I did. "If anyone would know about Mr. Tsow, it would be Auntie Ruby. She's a walking encyclopedia of gossip. If Mrs. Chin is her target, we should be safe enough."

She pointed a cane down the block—and nearly took off a man's head in the process. "Then it's on to Taipei Gardens."

When the light changed, we joined the surging crowd of shoppers with shopping bags full of Chinese vegetables and roast ducks. A similar mass had stepped off the opposite curb. Somehow the two streams managed to meet and flow through each other and keep hold of their bags of food.

When I had heard the name Taipei Gardens, I had been expecting it to look like a Chinese restaurant. Instead, we stopped by something with an elaborately carved sign that looked like a Thai temple. In front of it were columns painted with gold leaf.

I thought we had stopped at the wrong place. "Are you sure that this is it?"

Ah Wing laughed proudly. "The Chinese don't waste anything. This used to be a Thai place, but the hotshot owners spent all their money on fancy decor. When it went under, Chinese snapped it up and got the decor, too, for almost nothing."

When I glanced up at the signboard again, I saw that it truly was Taipei Gardens. However, the words had been painted on a board that had been attached to the temple carving.

And through the open window, I could see a Chinese cook. He was dressed all in white, from his little paper hat to his T-shirt and pants. His apron, though, was stained. He was busy making dumplings. To his left was a stove with big steaming pots.

It must have been a good place, because the line of customers spilled out of the restaurant onto the sidewalk. Through the open door came the most heavenly, mouthwatering scents.

Maybe it came from living in crowded Hong Kong, but my grandmother had never heard of waiting in line for anything. She plunged right into the jammed corridor.

"Better keep up with her," Ah Wing grunted to me and lunged after her.

I followed, trying to ignore the indignant stares. "Excuse us," I muttered over and over as my face grew red.

I caught up with them as they got to the head of the line. "There they are," Grandmother said, pointing her cane again. As they tried to avoid her cane, the group shifted like pudding being stirred by Grandmother's spoon.

As she stepped into the busy restaurant, I made a note to talk to her about the dangers of her canes.

The people at the head of the line glared at me.

"Sorry. We're just joining our party," I fibbed as I slipped past. I trailed Grandmother and Ah Wing down the narrow aisle. The walls had been decorated with more Thai carvings and gold-painted columns.

Grandmother finally stopped by a table set against the side wall.

"Mrs. Chin," Grandmother said.

Amy's mother stopped twisting her napkin nervously and looked up at us as if grateful for a distraction. "Hello," she said. She was hardly taller than Amy, but she filled out her blue brocade dress.

With her were two other women. One of them was introduced as Mrs. Li. She was a tall woman with skin almost as pale as mine. Her prominent cheekbones and small eyes and mouth emphasized the roundness of her face.

Auntie Ruby, on the other hand, was as chubby as

Mrs. Li was thin and as short as Mrs. Li was tall. She wore a bright fire-engine red suit, and she was loaded down with gold and jade in the form of earrings, rings, a necklace, and bracelets. Her cheeks, too, were rouged like ripe tomatoes.

Amy's mother introduced us in turn to her companions. Auntie Ruby studied me curiously. By now I was used to that because of my American looks, so I greeted her politely in Chinese.

Auntie Ruby nodded approvingly. "And what was the name of the last dynasty in China?" she asked. She had a slight English accent like Grandmother and Mrs. Chin.

"Pardon me?" I asked.

"Quick, child. Either you know or you don't know," she snapped.

"Well," I said, trying to remember Grandmother's lessons, "the last dynasty was the Ching, but they weren't Chinese. They were Manchus who had conquered China."

Auntie Ruby lifted a finger as she corrected me. "Barbarian Manchus," she said. "What is photosynthesis?"

Fortunately, we had studied that in school. "It's the process by which a plant turns sunlight into food."

She seemed to be checking off items on an exam sheet. "And the square root of 169?"

I turned, puzzled, to Grandmother, who simply nodded for me to answer if I could. It took me a moment, but I said, "Thirteen."

I seemed to have passed some kind of test. Auntie Ruby turned eagerly to Mrs. Li. "She has intelligence as well as beauty."

Mrs. Chin gave me an apologetic smile—though I couldn't think why—and then she quickly looked away and said, "Robin studies ballet with my daughter, Amy."

"Ballet, Mrs. Li," Auntie Ruby murmured.

"Turn around, girl," Mrs. Li ordered. She had a slight northern accent.

"I beg your pardon?" I asked. I couldn't understand the point of this quiz.

"Please do as she says," Grandmother encouraged.

If we were ever going to find out more about Mr. Tsow, I guess I was going to have to keep Auntie Ruby and her friend in a good mood, so I pivoted slowly.

Auntie Ruby nudged Mrs. Li. "You see. It's just what I said. Ballet develops grace in a girl."

Mrs. Li leaned over and actually pinched my calf.

"Hey," I protested, jumping back.

"But she has calves like a dock worker," Mrs. Li said.

I was going to protest further, but from the corner of my eye I saw Grandmother shake her head.

Auntie Ruby patted Mrs. Li's arm familiarly. "It's a sign she's healthy. Young men don't want a weak little stick of a girl anymore."

"I don't know," Mrs. Li said doubtfully as she continued to inspect me for defects.

Auntie Ruby elbowed Mrs. Li. "Nowadays, you're

lucky if the boy doesn't bring home a girl with nose rings and tattoos."

"Times have changed," Grandmother chimed in. "And so have tastes."

"Just so," Auntie Ruby said and smiled at Grandmother in gratitude. "Won't you join us?"

However, the table could only seat four. "I don't think there's room," Grandmother said.

That didn't stop Auntie Ruby, though. She glanced over at a large circular table where there was a family of nine. In the center, on the round lazy susan were a lot of empty plates and platters. "Ah Tong, are you finished?"

A man turned around. "Auntie Ruby, I thought I heard you."

They chatted for a little bit and the upshot was that the family got up and filed out as Ah Tong paid the bill.

As we started to sit down, though, the hostess, a small thin woman in glasses, came over. "Wait. Wait. That's for another group."

Auntie Ruby beamed at her. "But these are old friends I haven't seen in such a long time." She worked her charm on the hostess as well, and we wound up at the big table.

In no time, Auntie Ruby had gotten busboys to clear and clean our table, and then she got a waiter.

As she was expanding her order to include us, Mrs. Chin leaned over to me and whispered, "I'm so sorry, Robin. I should have been suspicious when Auntie Ruby invited me to lunch. She never does anything for free."

"It's all right," I whispered back. "She just seems a little . . . um . . . eccentric."

"You watch it," Mrs. Chin warned me, "or she'll be trying to matchmake you, too."

"Too?" I gasped. "You mean she's trying to find a match for someone?"

"My Amy and Mrs. Li's nephew," Mrs. Chin explained. "He went to a ballet once, so Auntie Ruby seems to think a ballerina is a perfect match for him."

"But that's preposterous." I couldn't help laughing.

Mrs. Chin gave a little sniff. "Tell that to Auntie Ruby. She's as relentless as a crocodile. Don't say I didn't warn you."

I wondered if Amy knew. Probably not or she would never have let her mother go to lunch. Certainly she would never have passed on the location of the meeting to anyone else, even Grandmother. Was I going to tease her when I saw her again.

When Auntie Ruby had sent the waiter off with new instructions, she turned back to us. "Have you ever had a northern-style lunch?" she asked us and didn't wait for an answer. "They grow more wheat than rice so it's quite different. Wouldn't you say, Mrs. Li?" she asked her and went right on without waiting for a response. "I wish I'd had more northern food when I was younger. North, south, it's all Chinese. Just like us."

"I still think home cooking is best," Mrs. Li said. "And I think my nephew would prefer that cooking to be northern style."

"Nonsense," Auntie Ruby insisted. "Now that he's in America, he's going to want to sample everything. I've known Chinese who have lost their taste for Chinese food. All they want now is spaghetti. Can you imagine?"

I wasn't sure if she was really talking about cuisine or someone Chinese dating an Italian. Since my father wasn't Chinese, I felt I ought to defend not only other cuisines, but other relationships.

"Well, at least it's noodles," I said.

It was a mistake calling attention to myself, because that put me back into Auntie Ruby's sights. "You like Chinese food, don't you, Robin?" she asked.

I squirmed, beginning to feel uncomfortable. Despite Mrs. Chin's warning, I had felt secure from Auntie Ruby's clutches, but apparently nobody was safe.

"Sometimes," I said hastily. "But I like other things, too."

"So do you cook southern style?" Mrs. Li asked.

"No," I lied, "I'm a lousy cook."

Actually, I did my own share of cooking, both American and southern Chinese style. I glanced at Grandmother, desperate for her not to correct me. She gave me a sympathetic smile.

"Yes," Grandmother fibbed, "she's hopeless at cooking. Robin burns water. I've given up teaching her."

"Eating out is expensive," Mrs. Li sniffed disapprovingly.

When Auntie Ruby gripped my wrist, I began to feel

like I was on one of those nature shows where an antelope has a leg in a crocodile's jaws and is being drawn into the river.

"But Mrs. Li, look at how many cheap hamburgers Americans eat," Auntie Ruby pleaded desperately. "A young couple can eat out every night at the nearest fast-food place. And it won't cost any more than cooking at home."

"My nephew prefers northern Chinese food. I know his mother would be more comfortable with that, too," Mrs. Li maintained stubbornly.

Auntie Ruby let go of me as she shifted gears. "Then we'll have to see that he finds the best northern dishes," she assured her client.

Next to me I could hear Mrs. Chin sighing in relief.

Amy and I were both off the hook.

13

The Know-It-All

Some of the dishes in our lunch were familiar, but other things weren't. I'd never had onion pancakes before, but they were tasty. And the dumplings had a wonderful smell that made my mouth water.

It was a big feast, and Auntie Ruby seemed to be packing away most of it. Somehow, in between bites, though, she got all sorts of information from us—things like: when had Grandmother come to America and how much Ah Wing made. She could have taught the CIA a few things about interrogation.

I thought it was funny because we were supposed to be the ones pumping her for answers.

When she finally got around to me again, I told her a little about ballet. It made me a little uncomfortable because I could see her filing my answers away. The antelope hadn't completely escaped from the crocodile.

Even though I was a little nervous, we chatted politely

enough. And finally I got to the point of asking about Mr. Tsow.

Auntie Ruby frowned at my pronunciation. "Mr. Tsow? How do you spell it?"

"T-s-o-w," I said.

"No, no, how do you write it in Chinese?" Auntie Ruby asked.

"I think it's like this," Grandmother said. Dipping her finger into her cup of tea, she wrote out the Chinese character on the tabletop.

Mrs. Li and Auntie Ruby both peered at it closely. "Oh, you mean Mr. Cao," Mrs. Li said with a different accent and then turned to me with a patronizing smile. "In the new Anglicization, it's spelled C-a-o."

"Oh," I said in a small voice. Maybe that was the reason I hadn't been able to find anything in the library.

Auntie Ruby stared down at her cup of tea as she flipped through a mental set of data cards. "Oh, yes," she said. "Sad, sad," she said, shaking her head. "He was so famous, but that was his downfall."

"He had an accident?" I asked, trying to understand what Auntie Ruby meant by sad.

That brought more head shaking, and this time Mrs. Li joined in. "We had even heard of him on Taiwan. His Dragon King was famous."

"I saw him dance several times when he came to Hong Kong in 1964," Auntie Ruby said. "He was wonderful in *Swan Lake*, but he was marvelous as the Dragon King."

That was a new one on me. "What ballet is that?" I asked.

"It's based on a famous folktale," Auntie Ruby said. "It was set in a little village by the sea where a mean old rich man is going to force a poor girl to marry him. But the Dragon King heard her weeping on the shore and took on human form. And he fell in love with her and brought her back to his castle under the sea. She's frightened of him at first," Auntie Ruby explained and couldn't resist adding a plug. "It's what comes when a couple makes their own match."

"But she comes to love him," Mrs. Li said enthusiastically.

"But a good matchmaker could have smoothed things over for the both of them," Auntie Ruby sniffed.

Though I was doing my best to learn about my Chinese heritage, there were times like these when I realized just how little I knew.

"It sounds like Beauty and the Beast," I said wonderingly.

"Well, the Westerners got it from us," Auntie Ruby insisted. "Just like noodles and ice cream and printing."

I wanted to keep her from going off on a tangent, so I quickly asked, "What happened to Mr. Cao that was so sad?" I waited breathlessly.

"He was ruined by the Cultural Revolution," Auntie Ruby said.

"Like so many," echoed Mrs. Li.

After I had met Grandmother, I had been trying to understand more of my Chinese roots. However, since it covered over four thousand years of history and literature, I'd only picked up small bits here and there. I'd read a little about the Cultural Revolution. Back in 1966, Mao Tse-tung decided that his Communist revolution was getting stale. So he tried to start a new revolution within the old one by letting the radicals take over. They jailed and punished a lot of powerful politicians.

I wrinkled my forehead. "But Mr. Cao was a ballet dancer, not a government official."

"They went after artists, too," Auntie Ruby said. "As well as scientists and teachers."

"The radicals had so many targets that they enlisted young people in a new kind of army called the Red Guard," Mrs. Li added. "Someone your age would have had no choice about joining. You would have had to quit school—well, there would have been no school left because all your teachers would have been taken away. And then you would have been trained in the new revolution."

"The lucky ones went to things like jails for what they called reeducation," Auntie Ruby said. "But a lot of them were punished by the Red Guard. They were marched through the streets like criminals and denounced publicly. Or they got beaten up or worse."

I thought of the kids from my own school and gave a little shudder. They would have hauled out any teacher who had given them too much homework and humiliated them.

"But what did dancers do wrong?" I asked, puzzled. "We just try to give people pleasure."

"Dancers were also part of the elite." Auntie Ruby shrugged. "They were parasites living off the workers."

It was like hearing about a horror movie. In this case, though, it wasn't just a few people who were destroyed, but a whole nation. "So what did they do to Mr. Cao?" I was careful to give it the same pronunciation and accent Auntie Ruby did.

Auntie Ruby drummed her fingers on the table. "Well, I don't know all the details of what they did. I think he was paraded through the streets with a sign around his neck stating his crimes."

"What crimes?" I asked.

Auntie Ruby's fingers rubbed her lips as she thought. "I'm not sure, but it could have been because he had danced in *Swan Lake*."

"But you said he was good in it," I protested.

"Maybe he was too good," Mrs. Li said. "So people without such talents became jealous."

I shook my head violently. "I just don't understand."

Auntie Ruby swept some food scraps into a neat little pile. "You can't understand madness. But that's what happened in China. Professors suffered because they knew too much. Artists were punished because they were artists."

I stared at the pile of discards as if they were people rather than bits of our meal. Maybe that's what Mr. Cao had meant when he had warned me that the audience was just waiting to attack.

No wonder he had felt that way. If I'd had people turn on me that way, I would have turned bitter, too. However, something more must have happened to make him hate music and even the dance itself. "Do you know what else they did to him?"

Auntie Ruby raised her hand perpendicular to the table and lowered it like the edge of a knife. "They chopped off some of his toes."

I sat there for a moment, not believing what I had heard. "They couldn't have."

"Worse things happened," Auntie Ruby said.

As her words sunk in, my own feet began to ache in sympathy. From the expression on her face, Grandmother felt the same way. "Heavens," she said softly.

I felt dazed—beyond even horror now. "They took away the dance," I mumbled. That would be like clipping the wings of a hawk so it could never soar again. Or cutting up a masterpiece like the *Mona Lisa*. It wasn't about politics or reeducation. Politics come and go, but Madame had taught us that art lasts forever. Art is what makes humans special. And this had been a direct attack on it.

And Mr. Cao had lost his art just like the Beast had lost Beauty.

"A whole generation suffered," Mrs. Li said with a shake of her head. "And they're still trying to pick up the pieces."

And some of them couldn't. Like Mr. Cao. The Beast had almost died when he had lost Beauty. Mr. Cao had retreated into his own dark little castle instead.

I know how I had felt when I had to stop ballet lessons for a while. I'd felt like I'd lost part of me. I think I would have gone crazy if I hadn't been able to dance again.

Auntie Ruby and Mrs. Li went on about some of the victims from the Cultural Revolution, but all I could think of was Mr. Cao.

If anything like that happened to me, I would hide inside my dragon palace, too. And I think I would prefer fish to people as well.

Poor Mr. Cao. No wonder he was so fascinated by his angelfish. They had the grace and beauty that had been taken from him.

I felt like I had come upon the scene of a bad accident. You can see the car wrecks, but the victims have been taken away. But there are drops of blood, and you know something bad's happened. You just don't know how bad. What else had been done to him before and after they'd cut off his toes?

Auntie Ruby might still be going on about the terrors of the Cultural Revolution, but the waiter had brought the bill.

She glanced at her watch. "Oh, my, look at the time."

Then she made a great show of picking it up and totaling the dishes. "Yes, it seems right. Don't you think, Mrs. Li?"

Mrs. Li seemed surprised to be asked, but she took it. "I guess so."

"Please check the figures. They're usually right, but they can make an honest mistake." Pushing back her chair, Auntie Ruby said, "Now, if you'll excuse me, I have to powder my nose."

And even though the restaurant was crowded and the aisle narrow, she scooted out of sight to the rear, still leaving Mrs. Li with the check in her hand. She seemed to think Auntie Ruby was going to pay.

Mrs. Chin avoided eye contact with Mrs. Li. I guess she didn't want to get stuck with the tab, either. Instead, she turned to Grandmother and Ah Wing and began to talk about the upcoming recital.

"Amy's very excited. Night and day she plays a cassette of the music. How about you, Robin?" Mrs. Chin rattled on as she kept her eyes from Mrs. Li.

Mrs. Li still fanned herself with the check, searching the rear of the restaurant for Auntie Ruby.

"Yes," I said absently.

"Amy says your granddaughter has such an important role," Mrs. Chin said to Grandmother. "You must be proud."

"She never told me. She's so modest," Grandmother said, and turned to me. "How is that going?"

I thought about the stumblebum practice today. "There are some glitches. I've got a lot of work to do."

"You'd be suspicious if things went too smoothly right from the start," Mrs. Chin said.

The line waiting for tables seemed even longer than before. So the waiter came over to Mrs. Li. "No checks, no credit cards, just cash," he informed her.

Mrs. Li gave one last desperate stare at the rear of the restaurant, but there wasn't a sign of Auntie Ruby. Finally she made an exasperated sound deep in her throat. "Finding someone for my nephew has become very expensive. He'd better appreciate this," she muttered. Snapping open her purse, she counted out the money and handed it to the waiter.

I was beginning to figure out how Auntie Ruby survived without a salary.

I think Auntie Ruby must have been watching at the back of the restaurant. The moment Mrs. Li paid, she popped out again. "Oh, you took care of the bill, Mrs. Li? You shouldn't have. I'll pay you back."

"If you want," Mrs. Li said with a thin smile. From the way she said it, I don't think she ever expected to get back the money. "Now, if you'll excuse me, I must be going."

Auntie Ruby pulled Mrs. Li's chair away from the table as she rose. "I'll go with you. I just know we'll find someone for your nephew."

"There's no need to trouble yourself," Mrs. Li said. "I think we can manage on our own."

Auntie Ruby took Mrs. Li's arm. "What are friends for?"

Mrs. Li tried to pull free. "I really couldn't impose anymore."

However, Auntie Ruby held on to her like a limpet on to a rock. "Nonsense, I was put here just to make people happy."

And she was going to make Mrs. Li and her nephew deliriously—and expensively—happy, whether they wanted it or not.

Keeping a tight grip on her client, Auntie Ruby used her free hand to take a card from her pocket and handed it to me. "Here's my number, Robin. I know all sorts of respectable people who need good, trustworthy babysitters. Give me a call, and I'll arrange a job for you."

She was still attached to the unfortunate Mrs. Li as they waded through the crowd at the front of the restaurant.

As we got up, Mrs. Chin couldn't help teasing, "Better be careful, Robin. You could go to baby-sit a child and come back with a husband."

"Never," I said, tearing the card up into little pieces and stuffing them into the pocket of my jacket.

When we got outside, Grandmother sighed, "So that's what happened to him. How terrible."

"No wonder Mr. Cao hates everything," I said. "I think I'd hate everything, too."

Ah Wing tapped a foot in sympathy. "I would if it were me," he agreed.

"I don't know if he really hates things," Grandmother said. "I think he's just afraid."

As always, Grandmother put her finger on it. Mr. Cao wasn't a grouch, just afraid. So even if he could still paint and draw, he was afraid to do them much. I guess he didn't want a horde of children cutting off his fingers this time.

When I had first met him, all I had felt were the needles. I knew now that they were the quills of a porcupine. Underneath the sharp points was a soft creature—lonely and scared.

And so his kindnesses would have been small by other people's standards, but they were big for him.

Then it hit me: All this time, in his own frightened, angry way, he had been trying to protect and help me.

Finally I saw what Beauty had seen in her Beast.

I had no idea, though, how much it would hurt inside.

14

Lessons

"Ow!" Thomas yelped.

"Sorry," I apologized for the umpteenth time that Sunday.

"That's all right. Now my shins have a matched set of bruises." Thomas limped over to a corner.

Leah's practice room was fine for exercises, but it was small for a rehearsal—especially with Leah and Amy there, too.

"Poor baby," Leah teased as she held out a towel. "Why didn't you go out for something easier, like football?"

Thomas took the towel and began to wipe his face in exasperation. "At least I'd get to wear protection. Where's your head, Robin? On Mars?"

To tell the truth, I'd been thinking about Mr. Cao. "No, in China," I confessed.

Thomas plopped down. "What?"

"Sorry," I apologized, sitting down beside him.

He thumped his head against the wall. "No, it's my fault, too. I'm just so tired. I spent most of last night thinking about what I'd do if I couldn't dance."

Amy was rewinding the boom box. "You weren't *that* bad."

The thought of stumbling around during the recital made my stomach do flip-flops. "If we don't get any better, it will go from being hypothetical to real." I leaned my forehead against my knees as I thought about all the laughter.

Leah draped a towel over the back of my neck. "Hey, everyone goes through this in practice."

Thomas sighed. "No, Madame was talking to us about our characterizations. We're supposed to really be Beauty and the Beast."

Amy nodded sympathetically. "I've had to do the same with *Tom Thumb*. But that's easy compared to your story."

"What's the big deal?" Leah shrugged. "It's Beast meets Girl, Beast loses Girl, Beast gets Girl."

I shook my head. "It's about losing something. Madame said to make it personal."

"Like losing our dancing," Thomas added.

Even when I should have been concentrating about the recital, I kept thinking about Mr. Cao. "What would you do if you couldn't dance anymore?" I asked, lifting my head.

"Now that you've crippled me?" Thomas quipped.

Even on his deathbed, he'd be using his last breath to make a wisecrack.

I elbowed him to get serious—I'd had a lot of practice with that. "No, really. What would you do?"

My friends glanced nervously at one another. It was not something any of them wanted to think about.

Leah massaged her calf. "Well, I guess I could become a doctor like my mother."

I knew Leah better than that. "And you'd hate every minute of it," I said.

"Yeah," Leah admitted, studying her feet.

Thomas held his head in his hands. "I want to practice, not get depressed."

I could always count on good old Amy to listen to me, though. "I'll never give up on dance. If I can't dance myself, I'll always want to be near it. Even if it means making costumes."

Thomas pantomimed sewing. "Maybe you've found your future vocation." He rolled away from both Leah's and Amy's kicks, but not mine. With a groan, he lay on his back with his hands clasped on his chest like a corpse. "Now my ribs have bruises to match my shins."

Leah snatched up his towel and flicked it at him. "I guess I'd teach. But I'd weed out the scum like Thomas. I don't have Madame's patience."

Teach.

When Mr. Cao had offered to show me tai chi, he had been trying to teach me one of the tricks he had used to warm up for ballet.

In his own way, he had been starting to do what Leah had said she would do if she could not dance—teach.

And I had turned him down!

No, I'd slapped him in the face. I was as rotten as the children who had cut off his toes.

But maybe it wasn't too late. Jumping to my feet, I gave Leah a big hug. "You're brilliant."

Leah leaned her head back, startled. "But I'd teach only after a fabulous career of dancing, like Madame."

"You will," I said, starting to take off my pointe shoes.

"Hey, what about practice?" Thomas protested.

In most circumstances, dancing would have come first. But I knew I couldn't live with myself if I didn't make up things to Mr. Cao.

I couldn't wait until Monday, so I dropped by the Dragon Palace. However, there was only a boy of about eighteen behind the counter. I guess this was Mr. Cao's nephew. He had the radio on the same talk-show.

"What do you want?" he asked sullenly. He certainly had his uncle's winning personality.

"Is Mr. Cao around?" I asked.

"Gone," the boy said. "But he'll be back later."

Getting information from him was like pulling teeth. "Do you know when he'll be back, then?"

"No," the boy said.

I'd be surprised if there were any sales when the nephew was running the store.

Even so, I had to satisfy my curiosity. "Some people say the owner of this store is a famous dancer," I said.

"They're wrong," he insisted.

"Are you sure he didn't dance with the National Ballet of China?" I asked timidly.

The boy shook his head. "Never."

Grandmother and the others had been so certain, though.

"There was a dancer by the name of Cao," I persisted.

"Don't be stupid," the boy snapped. "There are a lot of Caos. All of them can't be him."

"Then what happened to the owner's foot?" I asked. I thought I might find out at least that much.

"It's an ingrown toenail," he said. "Now quit wasting my time. If you're not going to buy something, get out."

I couldn't very well ask him what his uncle's foot looked like. Well, I suppose I could have, but I already knew what the answer would be.

I put my hand in my jacket pocket and felt the bits of Auntie Ruby's card. When I got home, I reassembled all the pieces, but I still debated using her number. If I asked her for a favor, she was bound to ask for one in return. Then I felt ashamed. After all those noble words about helping Mr. Cao, I wasn't even willing to risk Auntie Ruby.

So I called her.

"Yes, Robin, I remember you," she chirped into the telephone. "You're lucky you called when you did. I was just about to go out with Mrs. Li. We're going to meet a new prospect for her nephew. I'm sure this will be the one."

I wonder if the new prospect knew how lucky she was. "Do you remember that dancer, Mr. Cao?"

"Yes, his Dragon King was one of my most cherished memories," Auntie Ruby gushed.

"Would you recognize him again?" I asked.

"I'll never forget him," Auntie Ruby swore.

"There's a fish store called the Dragon Palace." I gave her the address. "I think the man who runs it is the dancer. His name is Cao, too."

"Really?" Auntie Ruby asked excitedly. "Well, it means going in the opposite direction than I had planned, but I'll get right over there."

"He's supposed to be there sometime, but I can't say when. And what about your appointment?" I asked.

"For the Dragon King, everything else can wait," Auntie Ruby said.

It was another family dinner night tonight. This time Dad brought home a pizza while I made a humongous salad. As we chomped away, we tried to share what we were doing.

Things were crazy at work for Mom. Dad thought he had a line on funding for his next project: something about the life of a worm that ate radishes. It was a big ecological disaster. Ian told us all about his latest discoveries on how to get to the next level of the hottest video game. No one else had gotten that far. He didn't mention his mathematical studies with cards. I wasn't the only one in the family with a secret.

And then it was my turn. It was on the tip of my tongue to tell them about the Dragon Palace, but I knew they wouldn't approve.

Instead, I told them about what slow progress I was making learning the dance. And that seemed to satisfy them.

Ian was supposed to clear the table while I washed. However, he did it so slowly—one dish or utensil at a time—that I grew impatient and cleared them myself. I guess he had figured on that.

I had just piled everything into the sink when the telephone rang. "Robin," Dad called. "It's an Auntie Ruby."

In the living room, Mom groaned. Apparently she knew Auntie Ruby, too. "Tell her I'm not at home."

He called out, "She didn't ask for you. She wants Robin."

Mom came running from the living room to intercept me in the hallway. "What does Auntie Ruby want with you?"

"Just checking something," I said.

Mom wagged an index finger at me. "Just remember: You're too young to get married."

Laughing, I picked up the telephone. "Yes, Auntie Ruby." In the background, I could hear crowd noise and the clatter of dishes.

"It's him!" Auntie Ruby said excitedly. "He was just closing up the store, but I knocked at the door. And he answered. So I asked him for an autograph."

Only Auntie Ruby would be that daring. "And what did he say?" I asked.

She sighed. "I guess he wants his privacy now that he's retired, because he tried to tell me he wasn't Cao. But I never forget a face. When you help people as much as I do, you can't afford to."

"Thanks, Auntie Ruby," I said.

"No problem, dear." She added ominously, "I'll be in touch."

I was afraid to ask what that meant. I guess I owed her a favor now, and that's one thing Auntie Ruby would never forget. I hoped it would be just free baby-sitting instead of surrendering a kidney. But who could be sure with Auntie Ruby?

I couldn't worry about Auntie Ruby at the moment though.

Mr. Cao really was the Dragon King in disguise.

There were so many more unanswered questions and so much mystery about him. Yet he'd built such a thick, protective wall around himself that it was like a windowless fort. I thought of the former Dragon King huddling, frightened and angry, inside the darkness.

He had been concerned about my leg. And he had been kind to the little girl and to my grandmother. Maybe that meant the wall had developed a little crack. I'd have to see what I could do about widening that crack even more. I'd get him out into the sunshine somehow.

Becoming his pupil was the first step.

15

Roots

Monday, the lack of practice showed. We had a spectac-
ular spill when Thomas tried to lift me. As we untangled,
I murmured, "Sorry."

"I warned you to practice more," Thomas muttered.

It didn't help our nerves any that Ms. Stein was there.
She was a student at State and would handle the lighting and the music for the recital. She also would draw the
costumes that the parents would make and design the
sets that the parents would build.

While we practiced, Ms. Stein would mutter something to Madame, who would whisper back. And Ms.
Stein would make notes. I know she was just writing
down her ideas for the production, but it made me feel
awfully self-conscious.

At the end of the session, Madame called us over. I
was expecting a lengthy set of notes that would have ba-
sically told us one thing: We stunk today.

However, she threw out her arms and wrapped us in a big bear hug. "What's happening? I see you trying so hard. But it is like a broken toy."

Thomas glanced at me, and then bravely said, "It's my fault, Madame. I'll get it right."

I was feeling pretty tired and discouraged myself. "No, it's my fault."

Madame let us go and stepped back. "You are partners, so you share the blame. But today never existed. Wipe this rehearsal from your mind. We begin new tomorrow. Fresh. Clean."

I did a reverence. "Thank you, Madame."

As we went to our bags, Thomas whispered to me, "We should really work on it at Leah's. We don't want to stink up the recital."

He was right of course. But I kept thinking about Mr. Cao hiding in that cave with only fish for pets. I couldn't leave him like that. For the first time in my life, I'd found something that was as important as dancing.

"I know, but I just can't," I said to Thomas.

Thomas frowned. "This is important."

I fidgeted guiltily. "So is my job."

Thomas drew his eyebrows together. "There's nothing more important than the recital."

Part of me thought he was right, but the other part of me thought about that lonely Dragon King hiding in his cave. "You'll just have to trust me on this." I shrugged.

I was in such a hurry to get to the store that I pulled on my sweats over my leg warmers—even though it made my legs look like Popeye's.

"It'll have to wait," I said. "I can't skip work."

Thomas took out his wallet. "Five, six, seven dollars," he counted. "And I thought I heard some change rattling around in my bag. Couldn't you give that to your boss today and practice instead?"

"I'll meet you afterward," I promised. "Don't start without me."

"I'll try not to." He sighed as he put away his wallet.

When I entered the Palace, I didn't see Mr. Cao. When I shut the door, though, he stuck his head out of the back. "Oh, it's you." He disappeared inside. Apparently he was back to his grumpy old self.

I set my bag behind the counter and walked down the aisles to the back room. He was siphoning brine shrimp from the jar.

I nodded to the tank of his favorite fish. "How are they doing?"

Mr. Cao concentrated on the job like a surgeon. "They're fine."

In the awkward silence, I said, "I'm glad."

"Don't just stand there. Feed the fish." He paused and added, "And if any fool comes in asking stupid questions, just tell them you don't know."

"Stupid questions about what?" I asked. Mr. Cao was

so touchy that he might be insulted if someone merely asked him for the time.

He scowled, looking more beastlike than ever. "Some pesky woman thinks that I look like some silly dancer." He jerked his head at his bad foot. "As if I ever could."

So Auntie Ruby's visit had gotten to him. I tried to sound innocent. "Oh, are you?"

He lowered the tube in disgust. "Of course not. But try convincing that creature. The notion was fixed in her pathetic little brain."

"If she comes around again, I'll tell her that I don't know anything," I promised. I was sure Auntie Ruby wouldn't be back, so that was safe to do.

"Good," he grunted. "Well, what are you waiting for? The fish aren't going to feed themselves."

I thought I had glimpsed a crack in the wall Friday, but I'd not only closed it down by refusing his tai chi lesson, I'd sealed it shut by sending Auntie Ruby to pester him.

Had Beauty felt this bad when she'd come back and found the Beast dying? Nervously, I cleared my throat. "I was thinking about what you said the other day about tai chi. Maybe I should learn it if it can help prevent injuries."

He carried the brine shrimp over to the tank of his angelfish babies. "There are plenty of classes around."

"You said you'd show me a few things," I said, and held my breath.

He squirted brine shrimp into the tank. "What changed your mind?"

I told myself I shouldn't feel scared. After all, Mr. Cao didn't have fangs and claws. "It'd be handy," I said.

"You just want to get out of work," he grunted.

I kept control of my temper. Growling back at him would just make him retreat inside his castle. And maybe this time he wouldn't come out. "You could teach me after my hour's up."

He watched his babies swirl frantically around the cloud of brine shrimp. "It would just be a waste of my time and yours."

I was feeling so bad. Who knows how long it had taken him to work up the nerve to make the offer, and I had refused. And now he was afraid and suspicious. "I'll feed the fish," I mumbled.

I had fed about four tanks when he came out. "Well, would you really try to learn tai chi?"

I held the box tight against me. "Sure."

"Then we'll start now," he said, limping toward the front of the store.

"I said we could wait until my hour's up," I reminded him.

He glanced over his shoulder. "That would mean I'd be stuck with you longer."

He sounded gruff enough, but I was beginning to learn he talked that way even when he was being kind.

"That's true," I said, trying to keep from grinning.

When I had put the fish food back, we went to the small clear area near the front of the store.

"Do what I do," he said. He spread his legs and did a

kind of half-squat. Then he began to run through a whole tai chi routine, his body moving with a fluid grace. Every now and then, when a movement depended on his bad foot, it threw him off. And his awkwardness would make him give a little frustrated click of his tongue. I don't think he had done this in a while. Maybe because it reminded him of his bad foot. Still, he carried on.

When he was finished, he went into his stance again. "Now you follow me."

Of course I made a hopeless mess of it, so he stopped. I felt my shoulders tensing for all the insults. "I'm sorry."

Instead, though, he just shrugged. "I was worse than you my first time. We'll start with the basics, like the horse stance."

"Horse stance?" I asked.

He went into the half-squat. "It's like riding a horse, you see? Only you're not riding a horse, but the world."

"The whole world?" I asked, but I copied him.

"Good," he said and bounced up and down. "It's easier to be balanced this way. And yet you're very strong, too." He beckoned for me to come over. "Try to push me out of the way."

"Are you sure?" I asked. "You're always saying how clumsy I am."

"Even you couldn't hurt me," he said, taking a breath.

So I gave him a little push with one hand. It was like trying to shove at a tree.

"Use two hands." He grinned.

Even with both hands, I couldn't knock him over. "How do you do that?" I wondered.

"All the energy in the world flows like a stream, and that's what you ride." He gestured toward his legs. "You can root yourself like a tree."

I began to get excited because of Madame's favorite teacher, David Howard. "There's a dance teacher who talked about dancing as energy in your body. Maybe the tai chi could help."

"It certainly couldn't hurt," he said. "You'll be stronger and yet more balanced."

He sounded positive about that—as if he, too, had once felt stronger and more balanced when he had danced.

And he began the routine again. This time he seemed almost at peace. And that made it all worthwhile.

I can't say I was any better this time, but he was pleased. "I think that's enough for one day." He favored his leg even more as he limped back toward the counter.

So, whether the tai chi helped me limber up or not, I think it was a good start in helping Mr. Cao come out of his shell.

"You didn't wear yourself out?" I asked, worried.

"I'm only tired of your questions," he said, but he was smiling.

As an insult, it lacked his usual verve. Encouraged, I asked, "You know that dancer friend of yours? What sort of dances did he do in China?"

He rubbed his chin. "Are these questions just killing time until your hour's over?"

"You can stop the clock and start it up whenever you want," I promised him.

"Well," he said, "in China they danced both classic ballets like *Swan Lake* and *Les Syphildes,* and they also danced new ones."

"New ones?" I asked, curious.

"You heard of the Cultural Revolution?" he asked.

I nodded.

"Well, it was run by the Gang of Four. And they wanted new ballets. Some of them are based on history. There was the"—and he said something in Mandarin. "Let's see, in English, it's *The White-Haired Girl,* and then there was *Taking Tiger Mountain by Strategy.*" He grinned. "You would have liked *The Red Detachment of Women.* All the ballerinas carry guns."

I had never heard of those before, and yet it was part of my culture not only as a Chinese but as a dancer. "Tutus and rifles?"

"No, they wore a kind of uniform," he said. "And there were all sorts of martial steps. There was the High Tiger Pounce." He gave a little hop on his one good leg. "You jumped up on both feet and landed on both hands. Dancers used that in battle scenes."

"My brother would have liked that." I grinned.

"But the best one was the *Dragon King.*" His eyes were focused elsewhere as he remembered his own triumph.

I thought of what Auntie Ruby had said yesterday. "Was it based on a folktale?"

"And on history, too," he said. "All the ballets had to be partly about the political struggle of the masses. The Dragon King rescues a poor girl from a mean landlord— well, all the landlords were cruel in those days. But the girl couldn't enjoy luxury while her village was suffering. So she went back. When the Dragon King missed her, he took on human form again to help in the revolt."

I drew my eyebrows together in tight puzzlement. His *Dragon King* ballet was a lot different than Auntie Ruby's. "That sounds more like politics than a folktale."

"All the new ballets in China had to work in politics, too, even though they might be based on old legends." The corners of his mouth gradually began to tease up into a smile at the memory. "Even so, the scenes in the dragon kingdom can match anything in *Swan Lake*."

"I guess everyone gets what they want from a story," I said. When Ian saw me in the *Nutcracker*, all he thought about was the battle scene and the candy, not the dancing. "I would have liked to have seen the dragon kingdom."

The corners of his mouth drooped downward abruptly. "But that's what also made the *Dragon King* so controversial. Many people thought folklore was part of our heritage. But there was a radical group that insisted myths were superstitions that distracted people from the class struggle. So those scenes had to be cut."

I thought of the ballets I danced. "But if you take out the myth, you couldn't have *Beauty and the Beast* or *Cinderella*. Or *Swan Lake* for that matter."

"Then it's a good thing you weren't in China," Mr. Cao said grimly.

I thought I'd better change the subject slightly. "So how did they dance the *Dragon King*? Did they do it with traditional Chinese dance styles?"

"Oh, no," Mr. Cao said, scandalized, "they used the classic Russian choreography. But with some slight changes. For instance, a dancer doesn't enter in a direct straight line." He limped a few steps in a direct path. "Instead, they come in like this."

He walked awkwardly in a shallow curve, then changed direction and curved in the opposite way so that his pathway looked like a series of curves.

I watched fascinated. I felt like I was with Grandmother when she opened up a window on another world. "Why?" I asked.

He shrugged. "How should I know? My friend just said that they did. But maybe it's because there's no one straight, true path in life."

"Maybe life is a lot of little detours," I added.

"And they never just point like this." He thrust his hand forward, his index finger extended. "Because for every action, there has to be an opposite reaction like this." He folded his arm across his chest so his finger was pointing behind him. Then he raised his arm in a huge arc to point forward.

I couldn't resist teasing him. "You seem to have picked up a lot from your friend."

He lowered his arm sheepishly. "He talked too much."

Suddenly my eye caught sight of the hour. "Oh, I'd better feed the fish. I bet they're starving."

"Don't bother," he said. "Your time's up."

So he'd let me stay on the clock after all. "I don't want to cheat you. I'll give you your money's worth."

He got a box of fish food and gave it a jiggle. "You still feed them too much. I'd better do it today."

I thought of Thomas waiting at Leah's. After the last disastrous rehearsal, I'd better accept Mr. Cao's offer. "I'm sorry. I'll make it up to you tomorrow."

"Ah, well," he said as if embarrassed and then gave a little cough. "At least you try. And that's good. My nephew doesn't even do that much."

That was high praise from Mr. Cao.

I felt like the crack in the wall was growing wider after all.

10

More Lessons

Over the next week, I can't say I learned much tai chi from Mr. Cao.

Though I tried my best, I'm sure any tai chi master would have shuddered to see how terrible I was. The thing that amazed me was how well Mr. Cao kept his temper.

"No, no, embrace the clouds," he said to me one time, and he swept his arms out in wide arcs as if he were gathering a cloud into his arms. I attempted to reach out and hug a big, fluffy cloud, but from Mr. Cao's expression I could see it wasn't right.

"I'm sorry," I said. I waited for the storm to come.

I saw the old flash in his eyes, but he caught himself, and, to my surprise, he gave me an encouraging smile. "You're lucky that I'm not like my old teacher." He actually laughed and pantomimed someone swinging a stick. "If you made the slightest mistake, it was whack, whack, whack with the bamboo."

"That's terrible," I said.

He folded his arms. "But we're in America. Children here are spoiled. My nephew howls like a monkey when I just look the wrong way at him."

"Oh," I said, swinging my arms to keep them loose. "Did you try to teach him?"

"He didn't last five minutes," Mr. Cao grunted.

"I . . . I appreciate your trying to teach me," I said. His nephew, after all, was pure Chinese, and I was only half. "I know I'm not very good."

"You'll get better if you keep doing it," he said. "So when your three months are up, I won't want you to quit doing your tai chi."

I could feel my cheeks turning red. I would have probably done just that.

He looked at me levelly. "You have to promise to carry on. Otherwise, I'm just wasting time."

He used the same tone of voice that I had used with my family when we had made our contract to have dinners together as much as we could.

"I will," I said, hoping that I could.

I felt sorry for him, though, because he was stuck with a poor student like me. And yet he didn't seem to mind.

That puzzled me all that night, so the next day after practice I asked Madame why she taught.

"It is the true pleasure of teaching to watch a student grow," Madame said with satisfaction.

"But what if the student is so awful that she will never get any better?" I asked.

Madame smiled. "A student's development is the pleasure of teaching, but not the purpose. My teachers took time to pass on what they knew to me. And now it is my turn. Some students can carry away more than others. It is a debt I owed to my teachers."

So I guess Mr. Cao was teaching me for the same reason Madame did. And it didn't matter that I would remain terrible—which made me sad in a way. After all, Madame had good students like Eveline besides the bad students. All Mr. Cao had was me—a hopeless bumbler.

Of course, Mr. Cao, being the Dragon King, couldn't give up on zapping me. He just didn't do it as often. Maybe it was because I was getting to know the routine of the Palace and how he wanted things done.

And bit by bit I chipped away at the wall around him. More and more I thought I got to see the real person inside Mr. Cao.

Though he trusted me to feed the other fish now, he still fed his babies by himself. I can't say that I blamed him. They were growing quickly under his tender loving care.

Lifting the lid of their tank, he tapped the jar, sprinkling the surface with minute bits of food. He seemed almost happy as he watched them eat. I think this was the real Mr. Cao—the one before the Cultural Revolution had turned him into a beast. He could really be himself when he was with his fish.

And sometimes with me.

"How did you learn about fish?" I asked.

He chuckled. "I come from a long line of fishers. If you cut my finger, my blood would stink of fish."

I thought I'd do some fishing of my own. "So you learned about fish from your father."

He capped the little jar of baby-fish food. "These are all freshwater fish. He was a saltwater fisherman. When I was small, I used to go out with him on his boat when the seas were calm." He looked almost happy. "Just him and me, drifting on the sea. He had a good voice, and he knew a lot of songs."

"Do you remember any?" I asked.

He chuckled. "Most of them I couldn't sing for a young lady. However, there was one. How does it go?" He closed his eyes and then began to sing in a shy, timid voice—almost like a small boy.

The words were in Mandarin, so I didn't recognize them. However, the tune reminded me of a gull flying home over the sea. I thought of how I would like to look like that when I was dancing on the stage.

"That's lovely," I said when he was finished. "What does it mean?"

He scratched his chin with the jar. "Let's see. It's about a father sailing home to his child. He's happy to be going home, and he's urging his boat to go faster. So the boat does because the boat's happy, too. It's dancing over the waves."

"Did your father sing that to you often?" I asked.

Suddenly he looked so sad as he shook the jar in his hand. "I guess. That was a long time ago."

Why was it that even his happy memories led to unhappy ones? "Do you miss him?" I asked sympathetically.

"I don't know. I hardly remember him," he said. "In China, they inspect children at an early age for certain aptitudes. They thought I showed promise, so they took me away to a special school. It was all really stupid, and I hardly saw my parents."

"Not even on vacations?" I asked.

"I stayed at the school," he said, tapping his fingers against the jar. "And the few times I saw them, I had hardly anything to say to them. I was living in a big city, and they were simple fisherfolk. I'd changed, and they hadn't."

"How terrible," I said. So he'd even lost his family for dancing—and then had the dancing stolen from him.

"Life is a series of slaps," he said.

I thought I heard an echo of Mr. Cao's old growl, so I tried to shift over to a different subject. "What school did you go to?"

"Ping-Pong school," he sniffed.

"Did you learn to paint like that at Ping-Pong school?" I asked.

"We studied all the time," he said with a smile. "To be a good Ping-Pong player, you have to know a lot of other things like art and mathematics. So if we weren't playing Ping-Pong, we were learning something else."

It didn't sound like much of a childhood. He'd sacri-
ficed everything to be a dancer—and then had dancing
literally chopped away.

"Do . . . you ever have any regrets?" I asked.

I'd gone too far, though. He clamped shut again. "You
ask too many questions."

Still, I'd had my biggest glimpse of the person inside
Mr. Cao.

I couldn't give him back his childhood, but I was going
to do my best to make him realize his sacrifices weren't
all wasted. There are still people who appreciate beauty.

17

Crisis

That Friday, for the first time, Thomas and I practiced in pointe shoes. Somehow we managed to run through our piece without major mistakes. I can't say we were great, but we didn't stink up the place, either. I felt like we were on track and so did Madame.

"Good, Thomas," she said, clapping her hands together once. "I believe you are the Beast now."

"You always were," I murmured to him.

He just gave a throaty growl in reply. "Who wouldn't be, with a mortgage and a castle that needs new plumbing? Ow!"

Madame had pinched his wrist fiercely. "Be serious," she warned the both of us. "Do not play. You are not so beautiful and so beastly yet."

Thomas nudged me. "Beastly is what Robin is when she can't have ice cream. Ow!"

Madame had pinched his cheek this time. "I have not

killed a student yet, but someday, Thomas, you will make one joke too many."

Thomas retreated, rubbing his face. "Yes, Madame."

However, before we could start, the telephone began ringing. Madame nodded to her sister, who sat at the piano. "You'd better get that," Madame said to her.

As she scurried off, we went over to the barré to keep limber until our music returned.

Even now, after so many lessons, Madame still found something to correct. She put a hand under my knee to raise it slightly. "Remember, Robin. Sloppy warm-ups lead to sloppy dancing, and sloppy dancing leads to injuries."

Madame's sister hurried in and whispered into Madame's ear.

Madame scowled. "Busy. How can she be busy?" she demanded, glancing at her sister. "We are counting on her."

"On whom, Madame?" I asked politely.

"Emily. Ms. Stein," Madame said, crumpling up the note. "Keep warming up," she ordered us.

Then she stormed out of the room with her sister trying to keep close on her heels. I should have stayed with Thomas, but I was worried about Madame, so I started to drift to the door.

"Get back here. She'll blame me, and I don't want to get pinched again," Thomas hissed. "I've got enough bruises." He snatched at me.

Because of my little brother, I was an expert at dodging and kept on. I just had to know.

Madame had left the door to her office open. I could see her sitting at her desk with her back to us, on the telephone. Her sister hovered at her elbow.

"But you cannot just leave us like this," she said in an angry, worried voice.

I jumped when someone bumped into me. It was Thomas. "I thought you were afraid of getting pinched," I whispered.

"What bothers Madame bothers all of us," Thomas said. For once he was being serious.

"Yes, well . . . if it must be," Madame sighed and hung up. Her back was to us, but we saw her lower her head into her hands. "What do we do now, Ludmilla?"

I walked quietly over to the office and knocked on the door frame. "Madame, are you all right?"

Miss Ludmilla was going to close the door, but Madame motioned her not to. "Ms. Stein suddenly found a job on a production in Berkeley. She will have no time to do anything."

"So we won't have scenery or lighting." Thomas slumped against the other side of the door frame in disappointment. "I liked being in a production."

Madame pressed her fingertips together. "Even if it was a modest one?"

"But have you seen the eyes of the beginners?" Thomas asked. "They're so excited by it." I think all of us were, because we could pretend we were in an even bigger production.

I elbowed Thomas. We shouldn't be making Madame feel worse than she was.

Madame shoved the telephone across the desk as if it were to blame. "It is a terrible shame. I so wanted to give Eveline her chance."

"People will come to see her dancing, not her costume," I said, trying to cheer up Madame.

"But I have invited friends—" Madame stopped when she realized she had said too much.

It was too late, though. Thomas pounced on that tidbit. "What sort of friends, Madame?"

Madame rubbed the back of her head uncomfortably. "If I don't tell you, you will probably make up your own ideas. I have seen this happen in ballet companies many times. Dancers live on gossip more than food."

"If you don't want us to start false rumors, then please tell us the truth," I wheedled.

Madame shook an index finger at us. "You must not tell anyone. You swear?" When we nodded, she explained, "I invited some friends from the San Francisco Ballet. This is what I get for being too proud."

"Could they help Eveline when she auditions for them?" I asked.

Madame sighed. "I think so. I would put her in a setting like a prize jewel."

Madame looked so sad that I felt even sorrier for her. "But they'll judge her by her talents, not the scenery," I said.

"But there are many fine, fine dancers competing with Eveline for just a few positions," Madame said. "She needs every little bit of help. I wanted to . . . to . . . what did the newspapers call it?" She glanced at Miss Ludmilla.

"Showcase," her sister said.

"Yes, just so. I wanted to showcase her. I wanted to have the proper setting for the jewel," Madame said and cupped her hands in illustration.

It would be a shame for Eveline to lose her chance. For a moment, I was feeling even more disappointed.

Suddenly, I thought of Mr. Cao. I knew he could draw and paint, so he could do the costumes and set designs. He was familiar with ballet, too, so he would know what we needed. And maybe he had even picked up some of the more technical stuff during the productions in which he had been.

"Wait! I know someone who might be able to do the scenery." I ran back to my bag. His sketches were still in it, so I brought them to Madame.

"Good, very good," Madame said as she went through them. "But we cannot pay except for materials."

"He's not a professional," I said. Though, remembering the quality of the window, maybe he should be. "He runs the fish store."

Madame wrinkled her forehead. "Oh, does he have salmon? I love fresh salmon."

I laughed. "Not that kind of fish store. He sells pet fish."

Madame jerked her head up and down. "Oh, yes. I know the place. Such a lovely window."

"He did it," I said, feeling encouraged.

"Interesting." Madame flipped through the sketches again. "He would do fascinating backdrops."

It made me feel good to see how Madame's spirits had picked up. "And costumes," I suggested.

Madame set the sketches down on the desk. "Invite him to come tomorrow morning if he can."

We ran through the rest of practice, working on the transformation. When we were finished, Thomas asked me as I untied my ribbons, "Will that old grump help?"

Now that I had time to think about it, I wondered myself. The crack in his shell was wider now, but I didn't know if it was *that* wide. "It's worth a try."

Thomas folded his arms and tried to look his Beastliest. "Maybe I should stick around outside."

I jabbed him with one sweaty pointe shoe. "Why, Thomas, you're worried about me," I teased.

He blushed, but said, "A good friend would worry."

When I first started working at the Dragon Palace, I would have been anxious, too—but I thought I knew Mr. Cao better now. "No, I'll be okay."

I couldn't wait to get to the store. Mr. Cao, of course, was in the back room tending to his baby angelfish.

"Look," he said eagerly.

I peered at the tank companionably. "They have fins and tails."

"I should have a new batch of eggs soon. There's another pair of angelfish dancing," he said, turning to me. As soon as he saw my face, though, he said, "No."

I straightened. "How did you know I was going to ask you for something?"

He picked up a sponge and wiped at a wet spot. "Your face always says what you're feeling."

"We're having problems with our recital." The words came rushing out. "The regular person who does the costume and set designs can't do it. I thought maybe you could. You could come by our school tomorrow morning for the full rehearsal and maybe get some ideas for things."

He chopped at the air with the sponge. "I should never have done that window."

I hadn't expected him to give in right away. "We don't want anything fancy. It's just backdrops and costumes. You know. It's the school just around the corner."

Irritated, he threw the sponge down in the sink with a splat. "Why should I waste my time?" He jerked his head at the tanks surrounding him. "I've got the fish to tend to."

I began to panic. I shouldn't have gotten Madame's hopes up. I tried a dozen different arguments, but all I managed to do was work his sullen attitude up to boiling mad. "But I can practically see your fingers twitching to pick up a pencil and put it to paper."

He threw up his hands. "Leave me alone. Go to the front and do your chores."

When I first began working at the Palace, I would have been glad to be out of his sight. Now all it would do is give me time to think of how to break the bad news to Madame.

18

The Russian Draft

I wasn't up front more than a few minutes when Madame herself marched through the front door.

I was so startled that I nearly dropped the box of fish food.

"Ah, there you are, Robin," she said, spotting me.

"I thought you had rehearsals now," I said, clutching the box.

"I told them to keep warming up. This is just as important." She clasped her purse over her stomach. "It is important that we have a production, so I came to talk to our master painter." She pivoted slowly. "Where is he?"

I set down the box on the counter and went over contritely. "Madame, I'm sorry. I asked, but he refused."

"Maybe he does not understand," Madame said.

Mr. Cao must have heard our voices, because he peered out of the back room. "Do you want a fish?"

"No, I want to talk," she said, moving toward him. Madame had two kinds of walks—her everyday walk and her ballerina walk. The ballerina walk was a graceful glide that she used at recitals or when she was meeting parents or school patrons. Though she was a large woman, she seemed to drift light as a feather down the narrow aisles of the store.

It wouldn't have mattered if she had been the Empress of Russia. Mr. Cao was Mr. Cao. "Go away," he snarled. "I'm busy."

Madame put on a smile that could shake loose hundred-dollar donations from the stingiest miser. "It won't take a minute. My name is Madame Oblamov."

"I've got things to do," Mr. Cao said, and retreated into the back room again.

If he thought he would be safe from Madame there, he was mistaken.

She plunged right after him. "You are *the* Mr. Cao?"

"No," Mr. Cao snapped.

Over Madame's shoulder, I saw him changing the water in the babies' tank.

Madame craned her neck as she studied him. "I think you are him."

"You need glasses," Mr. Cao said, and clicked his tongue as water missed the bucket and splashed on the floor.

I tried to apologize to Madame before his insult upset her. "I'm sorry, Madame. I should never have mentioned him to you."

Madame held her purse in front of her like a plow. "It was an excellent idea. I looked at the window again. He will make wonderful backdrops and costumes." To him, she said, "So whether you are *the* Mr. Cao or just *a* Mr. Cao, will you help?"

"N-O." He wrote the letters with the plastic tube in the air. "Do you understand me? Nyet. Nein. Non. No."

Madame spread her hands. "If you are good at something and you do not do it, then you are dead inside."

Mr. Cao repositioned the tube so that the water spilled into the white plastic bucket. "Then you shouldn't be wasting your breath talking to a dead man."

Opening her purse, she held out a sheet of paper. "I have here a list of scenes. Won't you at least look at it? We only need backdrops for a few. And of course, costume designs. They must be simple enough for the parents to sew."

Mr. Cao took the sheet and crumpled it into a ball and threw it on the floor. "If you don't get out, I'm going to call the police."

Madame's nostrils widened as she sucked in a quick breath. For a moment, I thought she was going to lose her temper, so I put a hand on her wrist. "Madame, I'm sorry. He's rude like this to everyone."

"You do not know what rude is until you have tried to order a sandwich from a Leningrad waiter." Madame shrugged. "And I always got my sandwich."

Mr. Cao got an old rag. "You seem to have eaten more than a few of them."

I gasped in horror. "You take that back. Madame is a famous ballerina."

Madame held up a hand. "It is all right, Robin. Do you think this is the first time I have been insulted?"

Mr. Cao squared off with Madame. "All right. What if I was *that* Cao? I've got a store to run. Fish need a lot of attention. I don't have time to design costumes and scenery. Ballet is a waste. I found that out the hard way."

Madame leaned forward so she could look directly into his eyes. "Ballet is what makes life special." She reminded me of a show I had seen on PBS where an icebreaker lurches forward through a sheet of thick ice.

Mr. Cao tried to back up, but he bumped into the shelves. Madame had him cornered. "You wouldn't think that way if someone had done to you what was done to me!"

So he had finally admitted that he was *the* Mr. Cao.

"I can see you were injured," Madame admitted, "and for that I am sorry. But do you think you are the only dancer who had to stop because of an injury? And old age comes to us all and taps us on the shoulder to tell us we must stop."

He flicked the rag at Madame. "You don't understand. Why even bother with a recital? Deep down inside people are like wild dogs. They don't want beauty. They just want to attack."

I think if it had just been herself, Madame wouldn't have begged, but she was fighting for her student Eveline. And that's what made her such a great teacher.

"I care about the recital." Madame tapped herself and then flung out an arm toward me. "And Robin cares. And my students care. As long as there are a few of us, ballet carries on. Help us with our production."

He glared at her. "You think you know everything, don't you? Well, how would you like to have children with guns break into your home and drag you into the streets?"

"Is that what happened to you?" Madame asked.

He laughed harshly. "It wasn't the half of it. They made me wear a sign listing all my crimes—when the only crime I had done was dancing. Then they marched me through the streets. And the same people that had been cheering me onstage jeered at me."

"How did you get hurt?" I asked. "Did the children do that when they grabbed you?"

"The Red Guard," he corrected me. "They called themselves the Red Guard. No, that pleasure came later. When they searched my home, they found a paperweight—a present from a French captain I had met on a tour. And that convinced them I was a traitor working against the Revolution."

"But that's crazy," I said.

"It was a time when crazy was normal and normal was crazy," he said, echoing Auntie Ruby. "And so everything that had made me famous became evidence against me. *Swan Lake* was Western capitalist poison."

"But the Soviets danced it when there was still a Soviet Union," Madame said.

"By that time in China, Russia had become as evil as the West. There were skirmishes on the border between China and Russia," he said with a sour smile. "So it was a liability to dance in a ballet the Russians had taught us."

"But your other role, the Dragon King," I said. "That was Chinese."

"How do you know about that?" A light suddenly dawned, and he leaned forward. "You're the one who sent that nosy woman to pester me."

"Someone thought they recognized you," I said, backing up a step. "I was just trying to be sure."

Mr. Cao frowned as if he'd just bitten a sour lemon peel. "The radicals thought the *Dragon King* was just a superstitious story to please the middle class and delude the masses. China went mad. So much of its culture became just superstition that had to be destroyed. They even made puppeteers burn their puppets. So the *Dragon King* was a mark against me."

This was worse than any horror story because it wasn't just one victim, but thousands. "What did they do to you?" I asked.

"They sent me into the country to a farm for what they called reeducation. But all I did was listen to them rant when I wasn't gathering up pig droppings for fertilizer, I didn't join in. The children who were guarding me didn't think that was enough, either. They said I was too proud. They said a high-flying bird has to have its wings clipped."

I wished he would stop telling me one awful thing after another. "I'm so sorry."

"Not as sorry as I was," he said. "Even after those children chopped off my toes, I thought I could feel pain from them." He stared at the angelfish. "It's funny, but some nights even now I can feel them hurting."

I thought of my grandmother. "But you can't give up. I know a woman who had the awfulest thing done to her when she was a little girl. For three years she was in constant pain. And she's still in pain now, but she raised a family, and she has lots of friends."

"She may be a saint, but I am not," Mr. Cao said, unimpressed.

"I didn't mean to hurt you. I just wanted to help," I said in a small voice.

"It's a dirty, ugly world, bunhead, with dirty, ugly people," Mr. Cao growled. "No matter what any of us does, you can't change it."

I pointed toward the front where the tank of hermit crabs was. "You said the crabs change shells when they grow. Why can't people? You may not be able to dance, but you can paint. If you have a talent, use it to make this world less ugly."

Mr. Cao glared at me. "What gives you the right to meddle? For that matter, what right do you have to judge what I should or shouldn't do? That's just what the Red Guard appointed themselves to do."

"But I'm not trying to chop off a toe," I protested.

He ran his free hand over his face. "What else do I have to give up to be left in peace?"

The store seemed to be getting darker and narrower— like the walls were closing in. I felt as if I wasn't inside a room, but underneath a mountain that was going to collapse and trap me within.

What a sad man, and what a sad place. I'd just been fooling myself when I thought I'd cracked his shell. He wasn't in a shell. He was in a concrete tomb.

Madame, though, tilted back her head as she took a deep breath. "Did you dance just for applause?"

Mr. Cao stared at her as if she were a fool. "No, of course not. I danced because I wanted to."

"And your teachers," Madame coaxed, "did they teach you for the applause and fame?"

"They got nothing," Mr. Cao admitted. "Factory workers earned more."

"No," Madame corrected him. "They were able to pass their knowledge on to you. A dancer isn't like a writer or a painter when she does her art. When she's done, there's nothing permanent like a book or a statue. All that's left is the audience's memories of what she did. It's true you can videotape a performance; but it's even truer that the videotape is never the same as the actual dance. Dance is only a temporary art. It's like building a castle out of sand on the beach. One moment it's magnificent, and the next moment it's gone. And so when a dancer can no longer dance herself, there is nothing left to show for it—except to help the young ones. You owe your teachers that. Ballet is like family." She put a hand on my shoulder. "Whatever happened to you, do not blame these children."

"I won't help perpetuate this illusion." Mr. Cao flung the rag away.

Madame dared him. "Then paint. I am not saying this to you because of my recital now. I am saying this because of yourself."

"Of course." He smirked in a superior way. "Paint for your recital."

Madame stiffened. "Then do not do our backdrops or costumes. Paint what you like for yourself, but paint!"

"You don't understand," he said, shaking his head.

Madame folded her arms. "I do not understand your excuses and rationalizations. I only understand that you are wasting your talents. So you might not be able to dance anymore, but you have skill with a brush."

Mr. Cao shoved her away. "Get out."

I was afraid there might be a fight, so I pulled at Madame's arm. "We don't need scenery or costumes, Madame. We'd dance anywhere for you."

Madame put a hand fondly on my shoulder. "You see? This is why I teach," she said to Mr. Cao, and then she gave my shoulder a friendly squeeze. "I will see you tomorrow, Robin. Don't forget. Rehearsal begins promptly at nine. We have a lot to do."

Mr. Cao watched her leave. "Madame Bunhead is a funny old woman."

"You shouldn't talk about her that way," I scolded. "She danced in some of the biggest ballet companies in her day."

"And probably didn't understand 'no' there, either." He grimaced.

I admitted the truth. "Probably not."

He replaced the water in the babies' tank. "Will you be sorry you don't have scenery and costumes?" he asked cautiously.

I thought he might be having second thoughts, so I edged in closer. "I would dance anywhere, in any clothes. Don't you remember what it was like?" I coaxed.

When he had siphoned the old water out of the tank, he had sucked out some of the babies. I saw them darting around in the white pail. He began to vacuum them back up carefully and return them to the rest of their family. "Yes," he confessed slowly as he remembered. And for a moment I almost thought I had won, but it was only a moment. His jaw worked as the other memories came back—the nightmare ones. "But then I learned about the world. And so will you."

If I had thought Mr. Cao was really happy, I would have left him alone; but he was just plain miserable. He was just like his store, all boarded up with all the light shut out.

"What happened to you was awful," I sympathized.

"But aren't you doing exactly what the Red Guard wanted? They wanted to kill the dance in you. But I don't think they can. It's still in there."

"So what if it is." He pointed at his bad leg. "Look at me. How could I dance?"

"Dance isn't just being onstage," I argued. "It's the lighting and the costume making. And it's the sweeping up after. I love doing it all."

He jabbed the tube from the vacuum at me so close that it made my hair rise toward it. "You're too young to know what you're talking about."

"If you keep hiding in here, then the Red Guard have won," I pleaded.

I think that struck home, because he stiffened a little. But it wasn't enough.

"Why can't you leave me alone?" He winced.

If he had shouted, I might have stayed there and yelled back. But he spoke in a low, intense voice that was scarier than a holler. And his eyes . . . they looked so sad, so hurt, so scared.

I wanted to reach that poor frightened person and tell him he was safe now. However, all I could do was stand there. I had never felt so helpless.

"I'm sorry," I said.

He turned away abruptly, almost losing his balance because of his bad leg. He wound up gripping a shelf for support. "You have no right to judge me."

I guess I didn't. I'd like to think that no matter what,

I would stay with the dance, but who knows if that's true.

"You don't know what it was like," he said. "I had friends who died. Friends who committed suicide. Just by staying alive, I've beaten the Red Guard. Don't ask for more."

As I left the room guiltily, he stared at his angelfish, dancing in slow circles in the tanks.

19

The Artist

When I got home, I enlisted Leah, Amy, and Thomas in spreading the word that the recital was going to be a simple one. The important thing was not to make Madame feel bad.

We managed to tell most of the intermediate and advanced students. So the next day when Madame announced the news, we put on brave smiles. However, we hadn't been able to get in touch with that many of the beginners, and they made disappointed sounds. One little girl even began to cry, but Amy, who served as the unofficial mother to the beginners, managed to quiet her down quickly.

And then we all began warming up. It was our second full rehearsal, so the practice room was jammed. Thomas went right up to Amy and held up an arm. "Feel that muscle. I think lifting Robin is better than lifting weights."

"It takes one dumbbell to know another," Leah sniffed.

Thomas put a hand to his heart. "As always, I'm devastated by your wit." He started to warm up by rolling his head. "No onion omelets for breakfast, right, Robin?"

I didn't eat onions usually, but I knew it was Thomas just being Thomas. The more nervous he got, the more he teased. "No, I thought I'd have mercy on you."

I had just slid my foot out in a battement *tendu* when Mr. Cao walked in. I was so startled that I nearly fell over. As it was, I clung to the barré like a drunken sailor.

Embarrassed, he held up a small sketch pad to Madame. "I came to get ideas—even though I think this is all a waste of time because you're just going to throw my sketches into the trash can."

Madame smiled as if the storm yesterday had never happened. "I doubt that. I'm sure they will be wonderful."

Mr. Cao said something in Russian. It was hard to say who was surprised more—Madame and Miss Ludmilla, or the rest of us. He ended with a shrug that was a good imitation of Madame's.

With an even bigger smile, Madame said something in Russian back to him.

Mr. Cao laughed. "Please. Not so fast. My Russian was never that good. And it's been a while since I had to use it."

Madame chuckled with him. "Probably when the Russians were expelled from China."

Mr. Cao slapped his sketch pad against his leg. "That was forty years ago."

Madame rubbed her chin thoughtfully. "Could you do the lighting, too?"

"I can if it's simple," Mr. Cao said. "After a performance, the dancers and teachers and tech people would all get together and go over how things went. The tech people learned about dance and the dancers learned about technical things. And when we went on tour in the countryside, we were shorthanded, so the dancers had to do a lot of the technical jobs."

Madame held her hands over her head as if she were putting bulbs into sockets. "The lighting must be simple. We can only rent a few lights."

Mr. Cao didn't seem fazed at all. "Then it will be like putting on shows for the farmers. Sometimes there was barely enough power to run a lightbulb." He thrust out his chin defiantly. "But I draw the line at washing windows and cleaning costumes."

"We won't ask that." Madame chuckled. "Do you know the ballet?"

Mr. Cao nodded his head. "I've seen it."

"I'll write out another list of scenes for you," Madame said. She started to turn, but Mr. Cao stopped her.

"I have your list." He held up the wrinkled sheet of paper.

"Good," Madame said, "and I hope you'll also tell me what you think. An extra pair of eyes always helps."

Mr. Cao was surprised. "I wouldn't dare."

"It's not every day we have such a famous dancer visit us." Madame pointed at the piano. "You'll see best from there," she said, and nodded to her sister. "Ludmilla, a chair for Mr. Cao."

However, Madame's sister had already bounced up from the bench and was bringing a folding chair from the corner.

"Attention, attention." Madame clapped her hands. "Mr. Cao will help us with our recital. He is a world-renowned dancer, so I want you to give him the same respect you give me."

The beginners actually broke into a cheer, and Mr. Cao blushed as he lowered and raised his head politely.

Leah "accidentally" kicked me as she did a grand battement. "You didn't tell us he was a dancer."

"I didn't know until recently," I said in mid-plié.

Amy kicked me lightly from the other side as she did a *rond de jambe en l'air.* "Some friend," she sniffed. "I share all *my* news."

"He didn't seem to want people to know," I said uncomfortably.

On Amy's other side, Thomas leaned out far enough for me to see him. "See if I tell you when I work for someone famous," he teased.

I couldn't help going over as Mr. Cao sat down. "I didn't expect to see you."

He flipped open his drawing pad. "Don't get smug. It's not what you think."

He was reminding me of those old-timers in Chinatown. "I'm glad you're here."

He must have already gotten ideas just walking through the door, because he began to draw with a pencil. "I am not an artist. I'm a shopkeeper."

"Of course," I said, trying to keep from grinning. "You're just helping out a neighbor."

He glanced at me. "It's not that, either. This is the only way to get you to shut up."

"Thank you," I said. I couldn't resist adding, "If I didn't know any better, I'd say you were actually enjoying yourself for once."

Mr. Cao barely glanced at me. "Unlike some assistants, I only know one way to do a job—and that's the right way."

"I'm better when I'm doing something I love." I shrugged.

I had thought he was working on backdrops or costumes. When I looked closer, I realized he was drawing Madame's face.

It was just a pencil sketch on the back of a flier, but I saw her strong face and the lively eyes. There, captured within a swirl of black pencil marks, was Madame.

It was amazing to think one person could be born with two great talents. However, I didn't say anything, because I knew a compliment would only have made him snap at me.

"Robin," Madame beckoned, "you need to warm up."

"Yes, Madame," I said, hurrying back to the others.

While we rehearsed, I would glance at Mr. Cao. He was sketching all the time.

While things weren't perfect with the rehearsal, they weren't as chaotic as last week. It even made me hope that the audience might not laugh at us. At least when I had looked at Mr. Cao, he had not been grimacing, so we couldn't have been too bad.

Though he didn't say anything on his own, he did have suggestions for Madame whenever she asked him.

When it was my turn, I was pretty nervous. Thank heaven I didn't make any awful mistakes. When Thomas and I were finished, I checked Mr. Cao, but he was busy drawing.

"He's not smiling," Thomas whispered to me. He had been looking to Mr. Cao for approval as well.

"He hardly ever smiles," I said. "That doesn't mean anything." I hoped that was true.

Of course everyone watched when Eveline danced as they always did. She just seemed to drift across the stage . . . like an angelfish.

I glanced at Mr. Cao again. He was as awed watching her as the rest of us were.

By the end of rehearsal, we were all feeling tired but pretty good about the production. My friends and I got to teasing one another, so we were the last to leave.

Leah studied Mr. Cao from the corner of her eyes. "He doesn't seem like the monster you described. It must be you."

"She has that effect on people," Thomas observed.

"He's only kind to children," I said as we headed toward him.

At that moment Madame called to him, "We should talk over the production."

Mr. Cao's eyes checked the list that he had laid over one leg. "So you really are a dancer," he said to me.

"I'm learning," I confessed, which was the truth.

"You are good enough to get your own place in the recital," he said.

I shrugged. "Mostly I'm in the background."

"Not for long, if she can help it," he said as he closed his sketch pad.

And he was gone before I could ask him what he meant.

20

The Real Beast

I was surprised Monday when I saw Mr. Cao at rehearsal again. I thought he would have seen enough Saturday, but there he was—sitting on a chair next to Miss Ludmilla once more.

"Mr. Cao, what are you doing here?" I asked, stunned. "Who's running the store?"

He shifted slightly on his chair so I couldn't see what he was doodling. "I'm taking my lunch break."

"It's a pretty late one," I said.

He glanced at me and then his pencil scratched at his pad. "I've skipped a lot of lunches to work in the Palace. So I'm owed a lot of free time. Have you done your tai chi?"

I felt my cheeks flushing guiltily. "No," I confessed, "there wasn't time. I came here straight from school, and we're the first to rehearse."

He went on drawing. "Do it in the morning before school starts."

Fortunately Madame came over to him to distract

him. "I was thinking over what you said yesterday, and I think you're right," she said, consulting her notepad.

Since yesterday had been Sunday, when there hadn't been any rehearsal, that meant Mr. Cao had spent the weekend on our ballet.

As I set my bag down, I tried not to smile, but inside I was grinning because my guess had been right. Thomas was already at the barré. "What are you looking so smug about?"

"Nothing," I murmured, and began to warm up.

Mr. Cao glanced at Madame's notes and then at me. "Yes, she needs. . . ." He paused when he saw me eavesdropping. Then that awful man switched to Russian.

Madame looked thoughtful and said something back in Russian.

I nearly died from frustration as they carried on their conversation. That was a rotten trick. What did I need? A nose job? Deodorant?

Finally Madame nodded and turned to me. "Robin, we think you need to hesitate a beat at . . ." She glanced at Mr. Cao.

"Before you do the heron spin at the end," he said.

"Pardon?" I asked.

He tapped his fingers at the air as he tried to remember. "What was the English again?"

"You said it was the *grande* pirouette," Madame reminded him.

"Yes, thank you," Mr. Cao said. "I have two sets of names in my head for steps."

So Mr. Cao was not only working on costumes and designs and lighting, but the dance itself.

"Yes, Madame," I said as I limbered up.

They went on talking in Russian as Madame flipped back and forth through her notes.

Thomas leaned over to whisper, "So we're being watched by the Big Three. My palms are sweating. Are yours?"

I hadn't thought about it until Thomas called my attention to it. It wasn't so much Madame or Miss Ludmilla I worried about, but Mr. Cao. Saturday, he had to watch the whole company, but today, I would have his undivided attention.

We made it through the practice again without disgracing ourselves. Of course, there were the usual notes from Madame, and, when she had finished, she glanced over at Mr. Cao to see if he had any, too. "Mr. Cao?"

He shook his head. "I think they have as much as they can handle right now."

So we had a reprieve.

When I had done my reverence to Madame, I went over to Mr. Cao. "Did you want me to open up the store for you?"

However, he had already tucked his sketch pad under his arm. "No need. I'm finished here. Let's go."

Thomas hovered by the doorway. "How do you do, sir. I don't think we've been formally introduced."

"I saw you. You were the target for Robin's bag," Mr.

Cao said, but he shook Thomas's hand. "If you'd taken your punishment like a man, I'd still have my front window."

"I'm afraid that I've gotten good at ducking," Thomas said, weaving his head back and forth in illustration. "I've had so many rotten tomatoes thrown at me."

Mr. Cao laughed and clapped a hand on Thomas's shoulder. "I don't think you're going to have to worry about opening up a used vegetable stand. You're doing just fine."

My jaw nearly dropped open. Another compliment!

"Thank you," Thomas said, and shot a puzzled look at me. He had the same reaction that Leah had had Saturday: Mr. Cao wasn't acting anything like the monster I had described. Maybe now that he was back where he belonged, the real Mr. Cao could come out.

As we walked to the store, I couldn't help noticing that Mr. Cao had a lot more energy than before. If it wouldn't have sounded so odd, I would have said he bounced rather than limped.

"How are the sketches coming along?" I asked.

"I've done several," he said, hugging his pad against his chest. "But I had too many ideas for yours, so that's why I came today."

"What sort of ideas?" I asked suspiciously. I was afraid he might put us in clown costumes.

"I've thrown them all out," he said, waving his hand in dismissal. "I saw something new today."

"Sorry to put you to so much trouble," I said cautiously.

"You're not sorry in the least." Mr. Cao winked and waved a hand at the plywood. "And the insurance company's check is in the mail. We'll have light in here again."

I think there was already light inside the Palace.

When he unlocked the door, he limped toward the counter. "What do you think of this for your friend? The one who talks a lot?" The countertop was covered with sketches of costumes.

"You mean Leah?" I asked. "How do you remember her? You only met her that day I broke the window."

"I have the whole pack of you fixed in my brain." He hunted around through the stacks, shoving several aside until he found the one he wanted.

He had not only drawn a lovely fairy costume for Leah, but he had sketched her as well.

"It's wonderful," I said. And simple, too. My grandmother would have no trouble sewing it.

"And this is for your other friend," he said, searching through the stacks for Tom Thumb.

The costume was as cute as Amy. "And mine?"

He had a half dozen sheets in his hand. "These are all rejects."

"I'd like to see them anyway," I said, reaching for them.

He tore them in half before I could get them. "They're not the real you." He kept on tearing them into small bits so I couldn't put them back together again.

Suddenly the door banged open and a man charged into the store. "There you are," he said angrily.

I turned politely. "May I help you?"

The man was taller than Mr. Cao, but his face was similar. "What's this American girl doing here?" he demanded.

"She's Chinese," Mr. Cao snapped.

The man gave a short barking laugh. "She doesn't look any more Chinese than a fire hydrant."

Mr. Cao's face had changed back into the sullen mask. "Her mother's Chinese. So that makes her Chinese, too."

"That only makes her a mongrel," the man argued.

Mr. Cao balled his fingers into a fist as if he was ready to strike the newcomer. "You idiot." He waved a hand at the tank of his special angelfish. "Would you call those fish mongrels? No, they have the best features and that's what makes them beautiful and unique."

Normally I wouldn't have been happy to be compared to a fish, but I knew what those angelfish meant to Mr. Cao, so I knew it was a compliment.

The man didn't look convinced, but he seemed impatient to go on to more important matters. "What're you paying her?"

"Don't worry," Mr. Cao growled. "She's not costing you a thing."

He jabbed a finger at his chest. "She's distracting you, isn't she? That costs me."

"I skip plenty of lunches and work after closing," Mr. Cao snarled. "I think that makes up for it."

The man pointed at the door. "Then why was the store closed when I tried to drop by earlier?"

"I was . . . out," Mr. Cao said. He leaned against the counter.

The man strode over to Mr. Cao. "Doing what?"

Mr. Cao put his hands behind him to grip the counter-top for extra support. "I don't have to tell you my personal business."

"You do when it interferes with my store." The man caught sight of the sketches on the counter. "What's this?" He held up one sheet and then tossed it down in disgust. "Ballet! I should've known you wouldn't keep your promise."

Mr. Cao snatched it back. "I'm just helping out with a local school."

"Didn't we suffer enough for what you did back in China?" the man demanded.

He was as full of fury as Mr. Cao had been. "You were a dancer, too?" I asked.

The man jerked his head back as if I'd just called him the awfulest name. "No. I had the misfortune of being his brother. We lost our jobs, our apartment. . . . We wound up sleeping on cots on a farm in a barn."

"But you didn't do anything," I protested.

The brother curled a lip at Mr. Cao. "His stink rubbed off on me."

Mr. Cao paused as he smoothed the wrinkles from the pictures his brother had grabbed. "The Red Guard called the families traitors, too."

I looked back and forth between Mr. Cao and his brother. "That's horrible, but that's no reason to make Mr. Cao pay for it here," I said finally.

"Who do you think owns this store?" the brother demanded. "I scraped and borrowed and begged for enough money to get here. And then I brought over all my family." He glanced contemptuously at Mr. Cao. "Including this spoiled brat. And this is how he repays me."

I was beginning to understand the bargain. I bet his brother had brought over Mr. Cao on the understanding that Mr. Cao would give up ballet. Maybe that had been another reason why Mr. Cao had tried to avoid dancing and music. "You're in America now," I pointed out. "What harm can it do here?"

"This," the brother said, snatching up a handful of sketches, "won't put rice on the table."

"But—" I began to argue.

I saw Mr. Cao's knuckles go white as if he were in pain—as if his brother were chopping off another toe. "Never mind, Robin."

I stared at him, puzzled for a moment. "But you have a right to do whatever you want in your spare time."

Mr. Cao's shoulders sagged as if his brother had drained all the energy from him suddenly. He tore some sheets from his sketch pad. Then, turning slowly on his good leg, he limped along the counter, gathering up the sketches. "Here are your costumes. Give everything to Madame. I think these will help. I've done preliminary sketches of all the sets and most of the major costumes.

Madame should be able to piece a production together from them."

"But she's counting on you," I said, stunned. "All of us are."

"I have other people counting on me," Mr. Cao said as he held the sketches out to me.

I just stood there, unable to understand how he could turn away from something he clearly loved to do. "Why?"

"When you grow up, you'll know," Mr. Cao said softly as he stuffed them into my arms.

It sounded like his brother owned the Palace, so maybe Mr. Cao was afraid of losing his job. I guess that's what he had meant. At any rate, I was making him hurt worse. I felt an ache growing inside me.

So even though I wanted to argue some more, I made myself ask, "What do you want me to do? Feed the fish?"

"Yes, fine," he said.

I ran through my chores while he went over the books with his brother.

When I was done, I checked back with him again. "What would you like me to do next?"

"You can go," he said. He was looking very old and tired.

"Then what about doing tai chi?" I asked hopefully.

"That's all over. My brother's upset enough," he said, gently shoving me toward the door. "I was a fool to begin again."

I thought he was talking about more than the tai chi but ballet, too.

"See you tomorrow." I stowed the sketches in my bag.

It's funny. I had hated my job there, but now I realized just how much he had come to mean to me. And how much I was going to miss him.

"When are you going to get that dreadful monstrosity off my store?" I heard the brother say.

"In a few days," Mr. Cao said sullenly.

"No more drawing! No more painting! No more music! Just business! Do you understand me?" the brother shouted.

When I closed the door, I felt like I was slamming the door on a dungeon. The painting might be coming off, but the light was not going to come into the store. He was still going to be hiding in a corner, a dead man listening to other people live their lives over the radio. The only grace in his life would be the fish in his tanks.

I stared at the glorious painting. How could his brother call that a monstrosity?

I knew who the real beast was in that family, and it wasn't Mr. Cao.

21

The Debt

I found Madame and Miss Ludmilla still at the school in their office, eating a quick meal of piroshkis. "Yes, Robin. What is it?" Madame was slumped in her chair and her eyelids were drooping.

"I'm sorry for interrupting, Madame," I apologized. "Are you tired?"

Madame smiled wearily. "My students act like a tonic on me. They give me energy. When I am not with them, I become my age."

As I handed her the sketches, I broke the bad news to her. She took it a lot better than I had thought she would. Instead of getting angry, she shuffled through the sketches. "Good. Wonderful. Lovely," she murmured as she looked at one costume after another.

As I peeked at them, I had to agree.

Suddenly Madame lingered over one drawing and held it out to Miss Ludmilla. "This will be lovely. See the ribbons down the back? They will twirl when she dances."

Miss Ludmilla nodded in delight.

The beautiful costume had reminded me of something, and when Madame put it back with the others, I looked at it again. The ribbons down the back reminded me of the fins of an angelfish. I thought of the way his beloved creatures had danced within the water. Eveline would be just as graceful upon the stage.

Then I saw the face of the dancer. It was mine.

"That has to be a mistake," I said.

"No, here is your name," Madame tapped the bottom of the picture.

What had Mr. Cao said: the real me? Was that how he saw me? I felt touched and sad and unworthy all at the same time.

Madame set the costumes down in one stack. "And here's the scenery. Good. He has the dimensions."

I was puzzled by how calm she was. "You're not upset, Madame?" I asked.

Madame shrugged as she held up one sketch. "You have lived all your life in San Francisco, Robin?"

"Yes, Madame," I said, wondering what that had to do with things.

"Then you have never known what a real winter is." With the fingers of her free hand, Madame imitated raindrops falling. "It only rains here and the temperature stays at about fifty degrees. But in Russia, it snows and the cold can kill. All the complaints and tantrums in the world will not change the winter. So you learn to adjust to what you cannot help."

"I haven't ever seen snow," I had to confess.

"Be glad," Madame said, and turned to her sister. "Do we still have those spare boards?" When Miss Ludmilla nodded, Madame grunted. "Do you think there's enough to build a frame for the scenery?"

Madame's sister checked the sketch. Her lips moved as she added up the numbers and then nodded again.

"Good. We will start on it right away," Madame said as she pulled out a drawer and began to root around in the piles of junk. "Now where is the hammer?"

That alarmed me because Madame looked so exhausted. "I thought there was a parents' committee to do that."

"There is much to do, and we need a head start," Madame said, and made a disgusted sound. Taking off a shoe, she hefted in her hand. "Yes, this will do to drive nails if we cannot find the hammer."

"Couldn't it wait until tomorrow, after you've had a good night's sleep?" I asked.

"Sleep is for babies," Madame said, and waved her shoe at the stacks of paper on her desk. "There are a hundred little details to a recital—from the lumber and paint for the scenery to renting folding chairs."

I hadn't thought about that. "Just so we can dance."

Madame rose and put her hand on my shoulder. "Students like you make it all worthwhile."

Up until now, I had seen Madame's drive in the practice hall. She demanded and got the best from each of us.

I was beginning to realize that it spilled over into other parts of her life as well.

"Were you this dedicated when you danced yourself, Madame?" I asked.

Madame exchanged an amused glance with her sister. "You do not become a ballerina without it." Madame laughed.

I was still worried about Madame. "We don't really need sets."

"This isn't for me." Madame smiled.

I knew who it was for. "But Eveline wouldn't want you to go to all this trouble," I protested.

"What she wants and what she needs are two different things," Madame said.

And I saw that the dedication wasn't just to the recital or her school, it was to her students as well. "Yes, Madame," I said, and made my reverence with as much care as I could.

Only I didn't go home right away. Whenever I ran into things like this, I was so glad that I had my grandmother. Fortunately, she was at home and not off somewhere getting into trouble with Ah Wing.

"You're not researching," I said, nodding at the game station.

She held up her thumbs. "No, my fingers hurt. So I'm just enjoying my fish," she said, pointing at the fish tank over the television.

So I told her all about Mr. Cao. "He just caved in. Usually he's so tough—I guess he had to be to survive what he did. I can't see why he just gave in so quickly. Do you think he was afraid of losing his job?"

Grandmother folded her hands over her stomach. "From what you told me, he feels that he owes a debt to his family."

"But it wasn't his fault," I said.

"That doesn't erase the debt." Grandmother shrugged.

"Oh," I said in a soft voice. "It's a family thing." I chewed my lip. "But you should have seen him. He was so happy for once. I think he's really missed the ballet."

"The debt to his family outweighs the debt to himself," Grandmother said. "It outweighs even his own personal happiness."

I could see his viewpoint, but what about his family's? "But making him give up ballet is so cruel. It's as mean as cutting off another toe. And this isn't a bunch of fanatical strangers. It's his own family."

"Well, I don't know them. But possibly it's to punish him for what was done to them," Grandmother said. "He knows that as well as us."

I was shocked. "And he still goes along with it?"

Grandmother put her hand affectionately on my cheek. "Sometimes you're so Chinese, but sometimes you're so American."

I guess I was getting yet another lesson in being Chinese. "So that's what I'd be expected to do, too?"

"If we were old-fashioned," Grandmother reassured me, "which we are not." She pointed at her foot. "My parents thought that binding my feet would make me beautiful. But they were wrong. And I took off the bindings as soon as I could."

That wasn't until she was an adult. I remembered what she had said: "Even though the bindings kept you from as much pain."

"Well," Grandmother said, "you still dance even though your toes bother you, don't you?"

I wriggled them now and felt the pinch. "Yes, but it's nothing like you must feel."

Grandmother patted my shoulder. "Still, you put up with the pain, don't you?" Grandmother asked.

"I don't let myself notice it," I had to admit. "But I couldn't put up with what Mr. Cao does."

"It must be very difficult for him," Grandmother agreed.

I thought of what it had been like when I had to give up lessons. Whenever I heard a bit of music that I had danced to, it made me remember what I had lost.

"So maybe he wouldn't want anything that reminded him of ballet," I said.

"I would think anything that made him recall his famous roles," Grandmother said thoughtfully.

"Or even music," I said.

"Especially music." Grandmother nodded.

That's why he had kept his radio tuned to a talk station. And I had roared into his Palace and just started flinging painful reminders at him. No wonder he had been so sullen. "But why did he hire me, then? Why not just talk to my mother?"

She touched the bun at the back of my head. "Because you were a glimpse of his past. Maybe you even reminded him of himself at your age. Deep down inside, he didn't give up ballet. After all, the store is named after his most famous role."

My insides started to ache, so I wrapped my arms around myself. "We've got to talk to his brother and change his mind."

Grandmother shook her head. "No. He's made his choice, and you have to respect it."

"But—" I began to protest.

Grandmother wrapped her arms around me. "Robin, you can't save someone who doesn't want to be saved."

As always, Grandmother had left me a lot to think about. "The other person I'm worried about is Madame."

Grandmother patted my cheek. "Sometimes I think you worry too much."

"Only about the important people," I said.

Grandmother clasped her hands in front of her. "She's like a second mother, isn't she?"

I thought about that. Madame was special to me just like my parents and grandmother were. "I guess she is."

Grandmother nudged me. "I'll give you another Chinese lesson. Did you know in China that you can have more than one family?"

I scratched my forehead. "You mean if you're adopted?"

"Well, that's true. But I'm thinking of something else. There's the formal family into which you're born. But then in China there's also your school. Your teachers are also like your parents. And your fellow students are like your brothers and sisters. So they're all important to you. Which means you worry a lot."

"Well, I'm worried about Madame right now," I stated. "I think she's working too hard."

Grandmother sighed. "She's always like this before her recitals."

"Maybe you can speak to her," I said.

Grandmother spread her hands. "I've tried, but nothing is going to change Madame. That determination is what made her a famous ballerina, and it's what made her school so good."

"She's as bad as Mr. Cao," I grumbled.

"They're both dancers. What do you expect?" Grandmother winked at me. "And let me remind you: So are you."

I thought of those strong wills. "I'm not like that at all," I said, pressing a hand beneath my throat.

Grandmother chuckled. "You're just as stubborn as me—which makes you even more stubborn than them. Now help me make some tea, and we'll have some biscuits. There are chocolate ones in a tin."

That usually helped with most of my problems, but not today.

22

The Bugle Call

The next morning I woke up early and couldn't get back to sleep because I kept thinking about Mr. Cao and his family.

The Red Guard might have condemned him to a farm, but at least that had come to an end. His family, though, were going to punish him for life.

I had assumed he was the lord of the Dragon Palace when he was really the slave. All because of a debt he felt he owed his family.

As much as I tried to understand my Chinese culture, I knew I would never accept that part like he and Grandmother and my mother did. The Red Guard had stolen his ability to dance but his family were robbing him of the dance itself. That just didn't seem right.

I tried to think of other things, but the injustice just ate and ate at me. I kept tossing and turning, but I couldn't ignore the ache inside.

What was it Madame had said to Mr. Cao? Dance is a temporary art. When we can't dance any longer, we don't leave a shelf full of dances. What we can do is teach, though. However, Mr. Cao's family wouldn't let him do that. Not even tai chi.

That didn't seem fair. He should be allowed at least to pass on his tai chi. I got up and padded barefoot in the gray twilight to the living room. Mom and Dad were still snoring in the bedroom, and there weren't any sounds coming from Ian's room.

I'm not saying that I did my tai chi well. In fact, I was sure Mr. Cao would have winced, but for the first time as I did it, I felt as if my toes were reaching down deep into the earth. And my arms and legs were like the handles of a pump that drew the energy up into my body as it grew stronger and longer.

I felt like I was part of something bigger than me. You could call it Nature or the Tao or whatever you wanted. And it wasn't as if I had suddenly hooked up to it. The connection had been there all the time, but I had just ignored it. All I had to do was just turn on the tap.

I felt whatever it was fill me so that I became light. It's not that my body lost its weight, but when I moved, I knew I was part of a greater movement in the world— like being the little finger of some giant strolling along.

When I was done, I felt as refreshed as if I'd had tea and cookies with Grandmother. I wondered if this is what Mr. Cao felt.

When I went to school, I broke the news to my friends. "I think Madame is trying to do too much. I think we all need to pitch in."

Thomas saluted. "Yes, ma'am."

Leah elbowed him. "It will prepare you for your future career in painting walls."

Thomas patted her on the head. "At least I'll make enough painting walls to drop a few pennies in your cup when you're begging on the street."

Leah slapped her forehead and groaned. "I should have known better than to kid a kidder."

"You're the one who got him started," Amy pointed out.

Thomas threw an arm around Leah. "Yes, thank you. Thank you. I'll paint the sidewalk of your begging spot whatever color you want. Two coats even."

By the end of the school day, Thomas was very into his future job. "It's all marketing nowadays, so I'm going to rename all the colors: Pomegranate. Lipstick Red. Spruce Puce."

I tuned Thomas out as we walked to ballet rehearsal.

"Watch it!" a man snapped.

I stopped before I ran into a huge pane of glass that a pair of glaziers were holding. I was in front of the Dragon Palace. Several sheets of plywood lay discarded on the sidewalk. They were parts of the Dragon King, but the parts weren't in order, so his body lay to his left with his tail in the center and his head to the right.

It was as if they had cut up that wonderful creature. "I

wish I had someplace to store the painting," I said, feeling sad again.

Thomas glanced inside. "I don't see Mr. Cao."

I knew him by now. "He's probably in back with his angelfish babies."

At least they needed him.

When we got to the ballet school, we found Miss Ludmilla hanging a sign on the door. It read: CLOSED.

"What's wrong?" I asked her.

Miss Ludmilla turned around. "Poor Sofia," she said. Her voice was high and thin, so it sounded like a squeak. We hardly ever heard her speak. "I warned her not to go on that rickety ladder. But she wouldn't listen."

"What happened?" Thomas asked.

"She fell and hit her head." Miss Ludmilla bit her lip. "She's in the hospital now."

"Which one?" I asked.

"French's," she said.

"May we see her?" I asked, worried.

"I'm going there now," Miss Ludmilla said. Though she was tiny, we had trouble keeping up with her as she scurried to the hospital.

When we got out of the elevator on Madame's floor, we could hear Madame down the hall. "And I tell you, I must leave."

There was a pause while the doctor must have said something.

"There is too much to be done," Madame insisted.

Madame's sister bit her lip. "Oh, dear. Sofia will make herself even worse." She almost ran down the hall.

"Thank heaven you're here, Ludmilla," Madame greeted her as she went through the door. "Help me get my clothes."

Now that we were closer, we could hear the doctor. "You are not leaving that bed, even if I have to tie you to it." It was Leah's mother, Dr. Brown.

"I recognize that tone," Thomas murmured to me.

So did I. Dr. Brown used it whenever she grounded Leah.

"But there are rehearsals, and someone must coordinate the scenery and the costumes," Madame protested.

Thomas and I slipped through the door to see Leah's mother with her arms folded. She was the nicest woman when we visited Leah's home. However, with the white coat and the stethoscope, she had put on her professional manner. "Madame, you have a concussion. Plus enough nervous exhaustion to kill an elephant. You have to stay here for observation and rest."

Madame pounded the bed with a fist. "But nothing will get done."

Dr. Brown shrugged. "Then you'll just have to postpone the recital."

". . . postpone?" Madame's lips moved silently as if that notion were so absurd she couldn't comprehend it.

Dr. Brown sighed. "Madame, believe me, I know how

difficult that is. I don't look forward to having to explain it to Leah."

No, Leah would not take it any better than Madame.

Madame threw off her blanket. "I am fine. Thank you for everything. But now I will go as soon as I get dressed."

Dr. Brown positioned herself in front of the closet to block it. "You aren't leaving."

Madame swung her legs off the bed. "Then I will go like this. But I am going."

Worried, Madame's sister darted forward. "Sofia, get back in bed."

"Don't be silly," Madame said, setting her feet on the floor. "How can I lie on my back when there's so much at stake? I am like the old cavalry horse that hears the bugle call for one last desperate charge."

"Sofia," her sister said, "be quiet."

Madame sat there stunned. "What did you say, Ludmilla?"

Miss Ludmilla squared her shoulders. "I told you to be quiet. You must follow the doctor's orders. There are no bugles and charges for you."

"I can't," Madame insisted. "There is too much at stake."

"There will be other opportunities, but only if you be-have," Miss Ludmilla said. Bending over, she seized Madame's ankles and swung her legs back onto the bed. "And then you can charge whomever and wherever you like."

Madame looked past Miss Ludmilla toward us. "Robin, Thomas, help me."

I had never refused Madame—until now. "I'm sorry, Madame. You're more important than the recital. If you're worried about Eveline, don't be. She'd be the first one to tell you that you should rest."

Madame slumped back against her pillow. She looked from her doctor to her sister to us. "You are all conspiring against me." She pouted.

Dr. Brown covered her with the blanket. "That's right. We all want you around throwing tantrums for a long time."

Madame gripped the blanket. "I do not throw tantrums. I . . ." she said, squirming, "simply express myself."

"Yes, very forcefully." Leah's mother tucked her in.

"We'll spread the word among the students, Madame," I promised her.

"You will explain to Eveline?" Madame asked sadly.

"Eveline will understand," I assured her. Touching Thomas's arm, I led him out.

"I guess we'd better start making phone calls," Thomas sighed. "Want to split up the list?"

"Sure, but do you mind if I leave my half for later?" I asked. "I might as well get work over with." I wasn't looking forward to it now. It would be like visiting a prisoner in his cell.

Thomas glanced back at the room where Madame was again trying to wheedle her freedom from Dr. Brown.

"Maybe I'll stick around here for a while. I could fetch things for Madame."

"Or help hold her down," I said.

When I got to the Dragon Palace, the glaziers were caulking the newly installed panes of glass. With the lovely painting gone, the light flooded the store. Even so, it seemed cold and impersonal. It was just another place that sold stuff now. The Palace had lost its magic.

And when I went into the back, the Dragon King was just a man with a limp as he tended his angelfish.

"Shall I start feeding the fish?" I asked him from the doorway.

He glanced at a clock on the wall. "What are you doing here so early?"

I told him about Madame. "So I guess we're calling off the recital. I can come here right after school."

He seemed surprised. "Calling it off?"

"There's no one else to guide rehearsals except Madame." I shrugged, feeling another little sad twinge.

Mr. Cao smiled with one corner of his mouth as he remembered his own encounters with Madame. "I thought she was built out of iron. It's a shame. It was going to be a good production."

I'm glad he saw something in Saturday's rehearsal. I wouldn't have put money on it, myself.

"You don't know how much of a shame it is," I said, and explained about Eveline.

He shook his head. "That is a pity. She's ready."

He stared at the baby angelfish as they glided in a silvery cloud in the tank.

In the awkward silence, I added, "I did my tai chi this morning like you said to. And I really felt good."

He eyed me suspiciously. "It's not supposed to be a happy pill."

I felt my cheeks turning red. "I'm not explaining it well. I don't think I was doing it any better than before, but I felt . . . I don't know. . . . Like part of something."

He studied me and then grunted. "I thought you were just making it up, but that's the feeling." He added shyly, "I'd forgotten it—until I started to do it with you again."

I bit my lip. "I hope you keep doing it, then."

"I should," he said wistfully, but I knew he was worrying what his brother would say.

He looked so sad that I couldn't stand it anymore. "Your family should let you do that much," I blurted out.

He threw up his hands. "Always the meddler, aren't you? Can't you leave people alone?"

I decided to go for broke. "Not when they're miserable. Just how long is this debt supposed to last?"

He folded his arms. "That must be the American part of you asking. The Chinese part must know that a debt is forever."

"I guess I understand that," I admitted. "I just don't want to believe it. Didn't Madame say that ballet was like a family, too?"

"Yes," he said. He turned from me to study the fish as

they darted about in a silver cloud. "I'd forgotten about that relationship until Madame reminded me."

"Well, don't you owe a debt to them, too?" I asked. "You said yourself that you lived with them almost all the time. So in a way weren't they more family than your biological one?"

He didn't say anything. He just stood brooding while he tapped his fingers on his elbows.

I grew uncomfortable with every growing minute. Why did I keep making him so miserable? Maybe I should leave him alone like he had asked.

Finally I cleared my throat. "So what would you like me to do first?"

He pivoted on his good leg. "Get the key to the school."

"What?" I asked.

"I know enough of the ballet to hold rehearsals, and Madame can fill me in as I go along." He picked up speed as he headed for the door.

Apparently, Madame wasn't the only old warhorse in the pasture. Mr. Cao was already charging toward the front lines.

I barely backed out of his way in time. "But what about your brother?"

He paused. "Didn't you just tell me that I have other debts as well?"

I remembered what Madame had said. "To your teachers?"

He smiled sadly. "It's funny. When they took me from

home, at first all I wanted to do was get back there. But then . . ."

"Then you fell in love with dancing?"

He shrugged. "I wish my parents could have seen me dance."

"They never did on their visits?" I asked.

"It was vacation time at the school, so there were no recitals." He looked sad. "The ballet company did become my real family. As Madame said, I owe my ballet family, and that debt is even greater than the one to my biological family."

Alarmed, I warned, "Your brother will fire you."

He limped toward the front door. "I've got a little saved up. Enough to last until I find another job. In the meantime, I can direct the rehearsals until Madame can take over."

A responsible person would have stopped him. He was throwing away his job and his security and everything. But he was right. I was a bunhead, and proud of it. So was he. We were responsible to something else. I wouldn't have tried to stop him any more than I would have kept the Beast away from Beauty.

As we left the store, one of the glaziers called to Mr. Cao. "Do you want us to throw away the plywood for you?"

"Yes, and then lock up," Mr. Cao said. He looked so much taller and younger as he headed for the school.

The Dragon King was on the prowl again.

23

The Recital

I was all nerves before the recital. Leah had just gone on pointe, so we all had ribbons to tie. Amy and I waited for her to finish tying her ribbons. Then Amy said, "Now spit for luck."

She spat on the ribboned knots of her own shoes. Leah copied her. At first my mouth was so dry, I didn't have enough saliva, and I panicked for a moment, but I finally managed.

I peeked out of the dressing room at the auditorium. Mr. Cao was in back with the lights. I tried to give a thumbs-up for good luck. However, he was too busy fussing with his equipment. I guess he was nervous, too.

It's a funny thing about performing. You're so busy concentrating on your own small part of it—and trying to avoid making mistakes—that you never get to see what the audience sees. I could only enjoy it later when I watched it on Dad's videotape.

If I saw anything, it was the little mistakes people

made. The beginners were so happy to be onstage that half the time they forgot what they were supposed to do and had to be herded along. One of the newbies fell and scraped a knee. Amy hustled her offstage, and we took care of it before she had a chance to cry.

All my nightmares of this week came back—everything from breaking a leg onstage to demolishing the set. But as I began to dance, I felt all the practice and training take over as they always did.

It was funny in a way. Though I had kept doing the tai chi, I hadn't felt like I had that other special morning. Until now.

I don't mean to sound mystical, but I felt part of something bigger once more. Pirouette. Arabesque. They were steps that someone had created and generations had danced. And I was part of that, too.

No, I wasn't going to energize any light sabers or have special powers. I was just myself. . . . Small, insignificant, but light. And . . . happy. This is where I belonged.

Suddenly it was over, and as I stood there panting, I knew that, even if I was no Eveline, I had done my best. Dimly, as if from a distance, I heard the applause. The amazing thing was that it sounded like it came from more than my family, though I could hear Ian's whoops best. And I was sure Grandmother was leading the clapping.

Eveline, of course, was as wonderful as ever. I had all my fingers crossed for her as I scanned the audience for

Madame's friends from San Francisco Ballet. With the lights blinding me, though, I couldn't see any faces.

At the end of the recital, more applause rose big as a tidal wave and crashed over us. The beginners were hopping with excitement and pleasure. And even if the intermediate and advanced students were trying to act like cool veterans, inside we were jumping up and down just as much.

From the back of the room, Madame's voice boomed, "Bravo. Bravo."

So she had snuck out of the hospital after all.

Leah sucked in her breath and whispered to me. "My mother is going to have Madame's hide."

"Well, she has the scalpels for it," Thomas muttered.

Madame suddenly appeared, silhouetted against the bright lights. The clapping grew even louder from the audience, and we all joined in, too.

Well, at least Dr. Brown couldn't skin Madame while there were all these witnesses.

In her best ballerina walk, Madame glided to the stairs leading up to the stage. She looked well rested and as energetic as ever.

Behind her she towed someone—someone with a limp. Finally I recognized Mr. Cao's silhouette against the lights. He seemed to be struggling to get free, but Madame had an iron grip. He'd been in back running the lights while Miss Ludmilla handled the music.

We made way for them as they stepped onstage.

When Madame held up her hand, the applause gradually died.

"Thank you for coming tonight," Madame said. "But I especially want to thank one person—Mr. Cao. He is an old retired warhorse like myself. But he could not resist the call of the bugle. His charge won the day."

"You're mistaken, Madame. I don't run," he said, and good-naturedly pointed to his bad foot.

So he could even joke about it a little now.

There was laughter and even louder applause.

Afterward, the dancers mingled with the audience. I saw Madame with Eveline and her family and a well-dressed man and woman who I assumed could help her with the ballet auditions. I crossed my fingers and my toes for her and then made my way over to Mr. Cao. "You did it."

"We did it." He smiled. I was surprised when he hugged me. "And thank you."

So I'd helped a real Beast find his Beauty again. That was almost as good as dancing.

"You were great," Ian said as he came up. The stalk of the rose in his hand had gotten broken, so it drooped when he held it out to me.

"Thank you," I said, taking it. The stalk was sticky, too—I guess from the candy with which Mom had bribed him to keep quiet.

"You were lovely as always," Mom said.

"The costume helped," I said, glancing at Mr. Cao.

Mom gave me another hug while Dad circled us with his camera, trying for another one of his artsy shots. Sometimes I thought the camera was glued to his shoulder.

"You were so beautiful, you made me cry," Grand-mother said as she shuffled forward.

"Yes, great, great." Ah Wing beamed from behind her.

Mr. Cao eyed her as he tried to remember her face. "Ha," he cried, suddenly putting two and two together, "I should have known."

Grandmother smiled. "My fish is doing well."

Suddenly I thought of his other love. "What about your angelfish babies?"

Mr. Cao patted my head. "You've always got to worry about something, don't you? I bought the whole bunch of them and took them with me. My brother depended on my numskull nephew to put a value on them, but, of course, he didn't realize what they were worth. I got my favorite pair, too."

He was nearly knocked off his feet as a Russian ty-phoon crashed into him. "I can't thank you enough," Madame said. She gathered up Mr. Cao in her arms and swept him off his feet in a huge, crushing hug.

"We couldn't disappoint the dancers." Mr. Cao winced as his toes dangled in the air.

"You will help with other productions?" Madame asked, setting him on back on the floor.

He laughed as he adjusted his clothes. Madame's hug

had disarranged them considerably. "If I have the time. I'm the manager of the Imperial Seas—and earning twice as much." That store was just a couple of blocks away.

"You got a job already?" I asked.

Mr. Cao scratched the back of his head, embarrassed. "They were looking for an expert at breeding angelfish. It seems there's a huge market for them. And I've got a chance at becoming a partner."

I nudged him. "Your brother was cheap."

Mr. Cao couldn't help grinning. "He put my nephew in charge. We'll see if the Palace lasts even a year."

Having met the nephew, I wasn't sure it would last that long. "I'll bet it won't last six months."

"I wouldn't take that wager," Mr. Cao said, and then added, "Just do me a favor, bunhead."

"Anything," I promised.

"Don't swing any bags when you're in front of my new store," he whispered, so my parents couldn't hear.

Madame put a hand on his shoulder. "We will talk," she said, her eyes glancing nervously to the side. "Now, if you'll excuse me."

Madame scooted away in the crowd as if a fire had suddenly broken out. A moment later, Dr. Brown passed us calling out exasperatedly, "Madame, Madame."

"A manager with a chance of becoming a partner. How impressive," a familiar voice said.

Grandmother shifted on her canes. "May I introduce you to my friend?"

Auntie Ruby bustled up. "Everyone calls me Auntie Ruby. I've been hearing all about you from my friend." She motioned to Grandmother.

"Oh, really?" Mr. Cao said politely.

"And when I told my other friend about you, she just had to meet you," Auntie Ruby said. "Miss Lee. Miss Lee." She glanced behind her. "Now don't be shy."

She seized the wrist of a pleasant-looking woman of about sixty in a cloth coat with a huge metallic flower pinned to it.

"Miss Lee saw you when you performed in Hong Kong," Auntie Ruby said.

"Every night," she murmured, not daring to look up.

Auntie Ruby used her other hand to hook Mr. Cao's arm. "She absolutely *adores* ballet."

"How nice," Mr. Cao said, trying to pull free. "Now, if you'll pardon me."

However, Auntie Ruby's grip was as unshakable as a steel trap once she had caught her prey. "You two really have so much in common."

Mr. Cao swallowed. "Unh . . . really."

Auntie Ruby rattled on at a mile a minute. "Oh, yes— why, just the other day Miss Lee was telling me she had this extra ticket for *Grizelda* . . ."

"*Giselle,*" Miss Lee corrected as Auntie Ruby led the two of them away.

"See how knowledgeable she is," Auntie Ruby gushed.

"Unh . . . yes," Mr. Cao said.

Ah Wing shook his head sympathetically. "Auntie Ruby's got him square in her sights." There had been a dazed look to Mr. Cao's eyes—like a deer caught in a car's headlights.

"His head's going to be a trophy on Miss Lee's wall soon," Grandmother agreed with satisfaction.

Poor Mr. Cao. He might have gotten away from the Red Guard and he might have broken free of his family, but he was *not* going to escape Auntie Ruby.

For a moment I felt almost jealous. "Aren't you ashamed of yourself?" I scolded Grandmother.

Grandmother touched her forehead against mine. "It's time to let someone older take care of him, dear. He's not a pet."

I gave a start because I guess that's how I had come to think of him. A big grumpy pet. "No, I suppose not," I admitted. "Still, did you have to sic Auntie Ruby on him?"

Grandmother glanced at Ah Wing and whispered to me, "But she was so insistent, dear. And Auntie Ruby was talking about finding a match for me. It was either him or me."

"Let me introduce you to Robin and her family," Madame said. She must have eluded Dr. Brown once again. I turned to see the well-dressed man and woman to whom Eveline had been introduced.

"Robin, these are my friends, the Lewises," Madame said. "They wanted to meet you."

"You were wonderful, my dear," Mr. Lewis said, taking my hand.

"I'm sure we will see you on bigger stages one day," Mrs. Lewis said. She had a slight Russian accent. I was wondering if she had once been a ballerina like Madame.

"And this is Robin's grandmother," Madame said. As she introduced the Lewises to my family, I stood there in a daze. I wondered if they were being polite or if they had meant what they said. Could Madame have brought them to see me as well as Eveline?

I squashed that notion as fast as it had come up. I would be lucky to make the corps d'ballet someday, and yet I felt warm just with the hope. As I started to day-dream about a brightly lit stage, I felt sticky fingers take my hand. "I'm bored," Ian said.

Who knows what the future might hold for me? Whatever it was, I would always have my family to an-chor me. I wouldn't have to leave them like Mr. Cao had to do with his family. That made me feel even warmer in-side than my dreams.

"We'll be going home soon," I whispered into Ian's ear. "And then I'll play you a game of Wolf Warrior."

"I'd rather play blackjack," Ian said.

That would certainly get Grandmother in trouble. "Some other time," I said quickly, before our parents could catch on.

Ian arched a suspicious eyebrow. "Promise?"

"Promise," I swore.

Because no matter what happened in the next few years, I was going to enjoy my family now.

"Attitude, you two," Dad called. The camera was back up to his eye, and he was adjusting the lens.

And with a laugh, I turned with Ian to mug for the camera.

I wanted to remember this night always.

Afterword

Mr. Cao is fictional, but the excesses of the Cultural Revolution have been widely documented.

Some of the background—and the genesis for the Ribbons series in general—was a ballet movie that I worked on briefly. It would have been a joint American-Chinese ballet movie that would have been shot in China. However, as is the case with most movie projects, it never got beyond the starting gate. This book grew out of interviews and research I did for that project, including Lois Wheeler Snow's *China on Stage* and Beryl Grey's *Through the Bamboo Curtain*.